totally
free

LaureL shadrach series

2

totally free

stephanie perry moore

MOODY PRESS
CHICAGO

ISBN: 0-8024-4036-3

3 5 7 9 10 8 6 4 2

Printed in the United States of America

For my li'l brother,
Franklin Dennis Perry Jr.

The up-and-down relationship this character has
with her younger brothers
reminds me of the times you nagged me (smile).
No, seriously, it reminds me of how much
I miss the days when we were younger.
I'm so proud of the man of God you've become.
You never stress out, you take care of your responsibilities,
you give everything to God, and your heart is totally free.
I pray the readers of this work will
come away with those same principles.
I love you.
And remember, your big sister is always here.

contents

acknowledgments

I had a severe cold, but I could not miss my deadline. So what did I do? I took drugs. You know—Tylenol, Motrin, Nyquil, Sudafed. They worked for a few hours, but eventually I had to quit taking them. I had exceeded the maximum dose for a forty-eight-hour span. I learned a valuable lesson. I must take care of me. All I needed was rest. Though I'm not 100 percent, I do feel much better.

My situation reminded me of how easy it is to become dependent on substances. Problems can sometimes cause someone, especially a teenager, to want to drink or take illegal drugs to escape life's pressures. The message of this book, however, is that drugs and alcohol only bring temporary relief. To be totally free, you must turn your life over to Christ and rest in Him. He can handle any curveball that might be thrown your way. Don't yield to temptations. Be strong, be an example, be Christlike. Some of my characters suffer severe consequences for their sins. This is a novel, but you can still learn from them. Don't duplicate their wrongs. You can live a cool, Christian life as a teenager. Do it!

To all who are an important part of my life: my parents, Franklin and Shirley Perry Sr.; my publishing company, Moody Press, particularly Kathy Ide; my reading pool, Laurel Basso, Sarah Hunter, Laura Kasay, Carol Shadrach, and Marietta Shadrach, and ; my assistants, Nakia Austin and Rachel Splaine; my good friends, Chandra Dixon, Tawainna Bolds, and Tabatha Palmer; my daughters, Sydni and Sheldyn; my husband, Derrick Moore; and last but not least my Lord, Jesus Christ. Because of your support, this novel was written. Thanks!

o n e

ringing
the bell

d *ing dong!*
Things were going great until that moment. My boyfriend, Foster McDowell, and I had found our way back to each other, even though it was only through a phone conversation during my Christmas visit to my grandparents' house.

"Is that the doorbell I hear?" my boyfriend asked.

"Yeah. Hold on, Foster, OK?"

"Of course. Since you're in the house by yourself I will definitely hold on to make sure things are OK."

"You're so sweet."

"Go get the door. I'll be here."

"Thank You, Lord," I said. As I hurried to answer the door, I looked around at my grandmother's home, beautifully decorated for the Christmas holiday. Every single thing was in order, just as it should be.

My life was in order at that point too. My sprained ankle was feeling better, Foster and I were back together, my first-semester grades were great, and I had good friendships with Brittany, Meagan, and Robyn. I also thoroughly enjoyed being a high school senior.

"OK, OK," I said to whoever kept ringing the doorbell. "I'm coming!"

When I opened the door, to my amazement, I saw my family. Mom and Dad were front and center. My youngest brother, Luke, who was in ninth grade, stood on one side of them. My oldest younger brother, Liam, who was two years older than Luke, stood on the other side, grinning from one rosy cheek to the other. Behind them stood my grandmother and grandfather. They were all dressed in red stocking caps and green woolen scarves and were singing "Away in a Manger," looking just like the carolers you see on Christmas cards. I listened to the harmonious sound for a moment, then remembered my boyfriend was still on the phone.

"Thanks, you guys," I said, laughing, "but you don't have to sing to me. I already know how good you sound. Go to another house." I started to close the door.

"Where's the eggnog?" my father's father yelled from the back of the group. "Y'all dragged me out here in the cold. The least I deserve is some eggnog with a little nip in it. I should be able to get some from my own house."

My grandmother hit him on the shoulder, then led the group down the street.

"How's your cold?" my mother asked, hesitating in the doorway. "You seem to be feeling better."

"Yep, I am." I couldn't keep from grinning.

"Where's your brother? Have you checked on him?"

Since Liam and Luke were with them, I knew she was talking about my middle brother, Lance. I didn't even know he was home. "I haven't seen him," I said, rubbing my arms to keep off the chill coming in the open door. "Maybe he went out for a second."

"He said he wasn't feeling well; that's why he didn't come with us. But we'll be done shortly. We're going to sing

12

at a few more houses and then come back and make you two some chicken noodle soup."

"That sounds good," I said, then watched her join the others. "And you guys sound good too," I added before closing the door.

I fled back to the phone, only to hear a dial tone. I'd expected that, but it still broke my heart. When I tried Foster's number, the line was busy. Then it dawned on me that maybe he was trying to call me. So I hung up right away. As soon as I did, the phone rang again. It was Foster.

"I tried to hang on, but someone rang in on the line for my mom. I didn't hang up on purpose."

"I know," I said. "I'm really sorry. I didn't mean to take so long. It was my family at the door. They came caroling."

"So, how are they?" Foster asked.

"My grandfather asked for alcoholic eggnog. Isn't that weird?"

Suddenly I heard someone screeching somewhere in the house.

"What was that?" Foster asked.

"I don't know. My mom said Lance was here." The screeching grew louder. "I'll call you back," I told my boyfriend.

"No, I'll hang on until you find out what's going on."

Putting the phone down again, I went out into the hallway. "What happened?" I called. "What's wrong?" I hurried down the hardwood floor. When I turned the corner I saw a horrific sight. Lance was sitting on the floor, leaning against the wall, surrounded by shards of glass and a small pool of blood. My heart sank as I scrambled to him.

"Get back, Laurel," he shrieked, gripping his left arm. "There's broken glass everywhere."

Ignoring his request, I squatted next to him and peeled his fingers away from his arm.

"Ow!" he screamed.

Blood poured out of a jagged gash. Without really thinking, I raced for the bathroom and snatched a hand towel off the rack, then returned and wrapped it around Lance's arm. Within seconds, the blood soaked the towel, obliterating its peach-and-pink rose pattern. "This cut is really deep," I said. "We've got to get you to a hospital."

"No, Laurel," he said, staring at the floor.

"I've at least got to call Dad on his cell phone."

"No!" His body started shaking. He looked up at me. His eyes were filled with fear and his breath reeked of alcohol.

"What in the world!" I exclaimed. I stood, fighting conflicting emotions of concern and frustration. When my brother shrugged, frustration won out. I left him sitting there, howling in pain.

"You're not gonna believe this," I said when I got back to Foster on the phone.

"Is Lance OK?"

"I think he's drunk," I said. "No, I know he is."

"What was the screaming about?"

"He must have slipped in the hallway and cut himself on a wine glass he dropped."

"How deep is the cut?" Foster asked.

"I don't know. He's still screaming and I'm scared."

"You've got to get him to the hospital."

"That's what I said. But he won't let me." I started to panic. "Foster, I don't know what to do."

"Don't worry, Laurel," Foster said. "Everything will be OK."

"How do you know?"

"I'm going to be praying for you."

Immediately, my racing heart felt more relaxed. The situation hadn't changed, but just knowing that Foster would be praying gave me a sense of peace. "Thanks," I said.

After hanging up the phone, I returned to the hallway. *Lord,* I prayed as I ran, *guide my feet and show me what to do.*

I found my brother kneeling on the floor, trying to pick up some of the larger bits of glass. "I've got to clean up this mess," he said, his words slurred.

"That's not important now. First we've got to get you fixed up."

Fortunately I knew where my grandmother kept her car keys. As I started the engine of her brand-new Lincoln Town Car, I thanked the Lord that I had passed my driver's license test just before Christmas break. I still didn't have a car of my own, but at least I could drive other people's cars once in a while.

I drove quickly but carefully. I sure didn't want to get stopped by a police officer and delay getting Lance to the hospital by having to show my temporary license and my grandmother's registration and insurance information, which I hoped were in the glove compartment.

After a frantic drive to the emergency room, followed by a two-hour wait in the visitor's area, the doctor came out and told me that my brother was going to be fine. "Do you have his insurance information?" the doctor asked.

"Yeah, I do." I pulled out the family's medical card and he handed me a clipboard full of forms. I filled them out the best I could, then turned them in to the nurse behind the counter. When she asked me for the co-pay, I came up a little short. In spite of my brother's plea for silence, I had to call Grandmother's house.

My panicking mom answered the phone. "Where are you guys? We came home and found your grandmother's car gone. Then we saw blood all over the hallway carpet. Laurel, what's going on?"

I told her about Lance dropping a glass and cutting his arm. I didn't tell her about the alcohol I'd smelled on his breath.

"Your father will be right there," she said.

After hanging up, I went into my brother's room to make sure Lance was really OK.

"Hey," he said in a groggy tone.

"Hey yourself," I said, approaching his bed. "You scared me half to death."

"Me too. You know, I've been thinking about it, and I honestly don't know what happened."

"Lance, alcohol is what happened," I said, my voice stern. "Where did you get it and what were you doing with it?"

"I don't know. I just went behind Grandpa's bar and tried a little bit of everything I found there."

"Why would you do that?"

"It felt good. I was really relaxed." His eyes focused on mine. "Laurel, you can't tell Mom and Dad about this."

I felt my jaw clench. "I had to call them. The hospital needed a co-pay and I didn't have enough money to cover it. They're on their way here right now."

Lance's eyes widened. "Did you tell them what happened?"

"No," I said. "But I can't promise you I won't. They're gonna want to know."

"Just tell them I slipped. You know Grandma's floor is always slippery. Laurel, please," my brother begged me. "I've been there for you. Just be here for me this time."

I hesitated. He was right. Lance had been there for me. I immediately remembered one night during my junior year when he caught me at home alone with Branson, my old boyfriend, and I begged him not to tell our parents. He never did.

Being a teenager was tough for anybody. But being pastor's kids made our lives even more difficult in some ways. A lot was expected of us, by people in the church and especially those outside it.

"OK," I said tentatively. "I won't say anything."

Lance sighed and closed his eyes. He looked like he was about to fall asleep, so I crept quietly back to the waiting room. As soon as I got there, my dad rushed up to me. I didn't lie outright but I didn't tell everything I knew.

My father was relieved that Lance was OK, and he seemed to believe what I said about Lance's accident.

I led Dad back to Lance's room. As I stood there watching him hold my brother's hand, my mind flooded with questions. I wasn't sure if I had really helped Lance out by not revealing the complete situation to our parents. But I finally decided to leave it alone, at least for a while. It was Christmas and I wanted to relax a bit.

Still, I was certainly planning to talk to my brother about this. I prayed I hadn't done him more harm than good by keeping his secret.

"Laurel, get up!" My grandfather's forceful voice woke me before the sun had risen.

"What's the matter?" I asked groggily.

"I need to talk to you. Right now."

I rolled out of bed and put on my robe and slippers, then glanced at the clock. He had to be out of his mind. It wasn't even five A.M.

"Grandpa, I need to slap some cold water on my face," I said, heading for the bathroom sink.

"Hurry up, then. I'll be in the den. Don't you get back into that bed until we've had a discussion."

"Yes sir."

Lord, what is going on now? I prayed as I stumbled to the sink and ran the water. *I thought my life was finally on track. When Branson wanted intimacy with me, I stayed true to You and didn't give it to him. But then Brittany did, even though she was my best friend and he was my boyfriend. How Brittany and I remained friends is anyone's guess. And then You sent Foster, a great Christian guy, to take Branson's place. I almost lost him by putting pressure on him to have sex, but by Your grace, we worked that out. Now Lance is a drunk and Grandpa is yelling at me, and I don't know why.*

The cool water on my face helped me think more clearly. *Grandpa must know about Lance,* I realized.

As I entered the den, I saw my grandfather and Lance sitting in chairs, not looking at each other. Before I had a chance to speak, Grandpa walked behind the bar and pulled out three half-empty liquor bottles.

"These bottles were brand new and unopened before we went out Christmas caroling. What's the explanation for this? There can be only one. My son is spending more time pastoring that church full of hypocrites than spending time with his own family. He doesn't even know his children are drinking. Who is responsible for this?"

Lance started crying like a baby. "Grandpa, I'm sorry. I just wanted to try some. Please don't tell my dad."

Grandpa's face softened as he looked at Lance's bandaged arm. "Well, I can see you learned a lesson."

"Yes, Grandpa. I definitely did."

My grandfather turned to me. "But Laurel, I'm very surprised at you."

"She didn't have anything to do with it," my brother said.

"Don't cover up for her," Grandpa said without taking his eyes off me. "The first step in recovery for alcoholics is admitting that you are one." He got so close to my face I almost fell off the chair. "I can smell liquor on her breath now!"

"What are you talking about?" I cried. My grandfather had no right to accuse me of such a thing. Alcohol was his problem, not mine. His addiction had almost destroyed his marriage.

When I was younger, my grandparents got into a huge fight, and my grandmother started pouring liquor down the sink. Then my grandpa started smashing her china. They sent me out of the room, but I watched through a crack in the door. My grandfather nearly choked my grandmother. It was the worst fight I had ever seen.

I felt my cheeks turn hot and my hands tighten into fists. "You're the alcoholic, not me," I blurted out. "You have been for years! You monitor those bottles so closely you know if anyone has even touched them. No wonder your marriage is shot. Alcohol is ruining your life!"

As my words echoed in the room, I saw a look of dejection cloud my grandfather's face. Clearly I had crossed the line.

Without a word, Grandpa stormed out of the room. I stared at Lance, wondering whether our grandfather would tell on us and what our fate would be if he did.

"Now look what you did," my brother had the nerve to say. "Why did you have to do that? I told him you didn't have anything to do with it."

"Obviously he didn't believe you."

"I was handling things just fine before you opened your big mouth."

My hands clenched into fists. "If I would've let you handle things last night you would have bled to death on the floor. Show a little gratitude, huh? I'm covering your back. I didn't even have any alcohol, and now I could be in serious trouble too."

"For what?" he asked, peering at me.

"For lying, Lance. I didn't tell Dad the whole truth. I intentionally tried to deceive him."

Lance rolled his eyes. "You are so dramatic."

"Look, if you don't realize how serious this alcohol thing is, maybe I should tell our parents."

"I know how serious it is," he said, instantly changing his tone.

"Yeah, right."

There was no point in going back to bed. I tried to find my grandfather to apologize to him, but then I heard his car drive out of the garage and down the street. Though what I had said was the truth, I hadn't meant to hurt his feelings. Regardless of whether or not it was true, I shouldn't have spoken so disrespectfully to him.

I took a long bath, trying to think of the best way to apologize to my grandpa. As I was getting dressed, I heard my grandmother stirring in the kitchen. When I walked through the living room, my brother Liam stopped me.

"Hey," he said. I turned and saw him sitting on the couch with a Bible in his lap. "Want to join me in prayer?"

"No thanks," I said. Though I needed prayer, I didn't want to pray with him. Liam was totally different from Lance. He was a good boy, just like my father. He loved the Lord with all his heart and didn't care who knew it. He spent every minute of his day trying to serve the Lord.

Liam also had good instincts. He knew I was holding something back. "So I suppose you don't want to study the Word with me, either."

"No," I said, my words clipped. "Is that a crime?"

Liam stood. "Why are you so on edge, Laurel? What's going on? What really happened last night while we were out caroling?"

I shrugged. "You know perfectly well what happened. Lance slipped and fell on his juice glass. Why do you have to act like there's more?"

"Why do you have to be so defensive?" he asked, moving closer.

"I'm not defensive," I argued, taking a step back. "Let's just drop it, OK?"

Liam grabbed my arm. "There's something else going on." I pulled away and headed toward the kitchen. "I don't know why you're always covering for him," Liam called after me.

Breakfast was uncomfortable. Lance couldn't even hold his fork without shaking. He might as well have worn a sign around his neck saying, "I drank alcohol last night."

Out of the blue Dad asked, "Has anyone seen my father?"

I started to say yes, but before I could get the word out of my mouth Lance knocked over his orange juice. It spilled all over my mother's beautiful hand-crocheted tablecloth.

"Oh, my goodness!" she cried, rushing around to clean up the mess. "Oh, my goodness!"

Just then I heard the garage door slam and heard my grandfather's footsteps in the hall. I started to panic. "Can I be excused, Mom? I don't feel good."

"Sure," she said, distracted by her cleanup attempts.

"I don't feel too good, either," Lance added.

Mom paused in her sopping to look up at us. "Maybe you two should go lie down for a little while."

"Yes ma'am," I said quickly, getting up from the table.

"OK, Mom," Lance replied at the same time. We both fled out of the kitchen and into the corridor. "You might as well give it away," Lance whispered.

"We need to talk to Grandpa before he goes back in there," I said.

"You want to talk to me?" The bathroom door beside us popped open and our grandfather came out into the hall, surprising us both.

"Grandpa," I said, "I just wanted to ask you to forgive me. I was totally wrong this morning and I'm sorry. I was disrespectful and I said way too much without thinking."

His eyes narrowed. "Laurel, cut the bull. You aimed to be vicious and you were successful in hitting me where it hurts. Don't try to butter me up now just so I won't tell your parents. I'm not going to tell them, because I had a big part in the whole thing. If I didn't drink, then the liquor wouldn't have been there." He took a deep breath, as if the truth of his words had really sunk in. "Let me tell you something, Laurel," he said. "You were right. Alcohol did get the best of me."

It wasn't my place, but I blurted out, "So why is that stuff in this house?"

"Hey, I'm a grown man and I'm set in my ways. Besides, we're all going to die one day. I might as well be happy when I go."

I glared at him, making sure he knew I thought his explanation was nothing more than a lame excuse.

"Look, I can manage this. But you kids, learn from me.

Don't make the same mistakes I have." His voice cracked, as if he was about to start crying.

"Grandpa, I'm sorry," I told him.

"About drinking?" he asked, his voice soft but accusatory. My back stiffened. "I didn't touch your alcohol."

"I'm the one who's been drinking," Lance put in. "But I've learned my lesson. I'm sorry, Grandpa."

"And I'm sorry about what I said," I added.

"It's OK, Laurel," my grandfather said. "You just opened my eyes to reality." He reached out and hugged both of us tightly. I could tell he was fighting back tears. "OK, kids. Since it seems we are all feeling better, let's hit the road."

Three hours later, as my family was all settled in our van for the twelve-hour ride from Grandpa's house in Conway, Arkansas, back home to Conyers, Georgia, I looked over at Lance. He was asleep, but his face looked tortured. I hoped I had done the right thing by not telling our parents. I knew he would have done the same for me. But what if this wasn't the first time? What if he needed help and I denied it to him by not telling? What if he became an alcoholic and killed himself or someone else? I would have to keep an eye on my brother.

When Mom noticed I was awake, she said, "You know, Laurel, we never got a chance to thank you for being there for Lance last night."

"You don't have to thank me," I answered in a hushed voice, so as not to wake my brother. "I should have called you right away, but I panicked."

"I can't imagine how your brother slipped," my father probed. "I know it was a hardwood floor. But quarterbacks are not clumsy people. And where did the broken glass come from?"

I stared out the car window, not saying anything, hoping

he didn't really expect an answer from me. I didn't want to get Lance or myself into trouble.

———————————

After the ride home, I went straight to my bedroom. The next day, my friends Brittany and Meagan came over.

"So, you endured another long, boring vacation with your family," Brittany said as we sat around in my room. "I'm so glad my relatives come to our house for the holidays. And when we do go visit them, we fly instead of drive."

"Actually, it wasn't that bad," I said. The truth was, I usually enjoyed having family discussions during car trips. But I didn't admit that to my friends. "Especially since we have a TV in our van."

"Oh, yeah. Your van is like a house," Brittany joked, obviously preferring her brand-new Jetta to our big old van.

"Lay off, Brittany," Meagan said.

Ignoring the comment about our van, I asked Brittany, "Have you gotten your results from the HIV test yet?"

Dead silence filled the room. "Everything's going to be fine," Brittany said. "I feel great. As a matter of fact, I'm having a party to celebrate the new year and my good fortune."

"You're having a party even though you don't know your results yet?"

"Yes," she said with a quick nod. "I have faith. You should understand that."

"Britt, I'm not trying to be funny, but exactly what do you have faith in?"

My gorgeous blonde friend played with the hem of her short skirt. "Faith in the fact that I'm going to be OK." She looked up. "So, are you going to join me in my celebration?"

"I don't know. Foster and I plan to spend some time at church on New Year's Eve and then pray together at midnight."

Meagan and Brittany blinked at me like that was the stupidest idea they'd ever heard. I was disappointed with them.

They were supposed to be Christians trying to strengthen their walk with Christ.

"So you're gonna choose a guy over us?" Brittany asked.

I couldn't believe she said that. Only a couple of months ago she had slept with Branson Price, who was my boyfriend at the time. She had certainly chosen a guy over our friendship!

The hurt I'd felt when I found out about Brittany and Branson still stung. "I'll be right back," I said, then hustled to the bathroom.

Meagan followed me. "You've got to ignore Brittany. She really is worried about her results. The doctor's office called her three days ago and told her the results were ready. But she's been too afraid to go in and get them." Meagan gave me a pleading look through the bathroom mirror. "Please come to her party. She needs you there."

I turned and looked at my cute, redheaded girlfriend. "I really admire you for being a peacemaker."

She smiled. "Thanks."

We hugged and went back to Brittany. "Let's go to Party City to get goodies for your celebration," I suggested.

Her face lit up. "I'll drive!"

———

I wanted to be there for my friend on New Year's Eve. But I also wanted to follow through on my plans to spend time at church with Foster. I had to figure out a way to do both.

I could go to church for a little while and then head over to Brittany's. Foster could come with me. But my parents wanted me to be at church all evening. It would be hard convincing Foster and my father.

When I brought it up at dinner that night, Dad bombarded me with all types of questions. "Who's going to be at the party? Why don't you want to stay at church? When will the party be over? Didn't you have plans with Foster? Is he going too?"

Between bites of my meal, I answered each question until he ran out of things to ask. Then I turned to my mom. "It's OK with you, right?"

"You know, honey," she said to my dad, immediately starting to plead my case, "Laurel will be on her own next year. She's got to start making some of her own decisions so she'll learn to be responsible."

"Well, I don't think I want her spreading her wings on New Year's Eve."

"Dad, have I ever done anything crazy? I've been going out for two years and I've only missed curfew once. And then it was because Branson put me out on the street. Give me a chance here."

He threw his hands up. "Go ahead," he said in a dejected voice. "If my own daughter doesn't want to be at my services, it makes me wonder why any other teenagers would want to bother."

"Dad, this doesn't have anything to do with you or God," I assured him. "I love you both with all my heart. But this is something I want to do. It isn't a sin. I just want to hang out with my friends."

"Do your friends go to church?"

"Yes," I shot back, "just not 365 days a year!"

My father's face turned red. He rose stiffly and left the room, several bites of his dinner still on the plate.

"Laurel," Mom said, "you know it's wrong to speak to your father in that tone of voice." Then she continued in a whisper, "If you could come to the beginning of the church service that would be great. Since you're spending the night at Brittany's house, we won't have to worry about you being on the roads late at night. I think you'll be fine."

"Thanks, Mom." I jumped up and hugged my mother. "But what about Dad?"

"Don't worry," she said, patting my arm. "When he's cooled off a little, I'll talk to him. But you be sure to apologize."

"Yes, ma'am," I said with a grin, returning to my seat.

"So," she asked, "what are you going to wear to Brittany's party?"

I paused, mentally surveying my wardrobe. "I don't know. That's another problem."

"You know, there are still some presents under the tree," she said with a smile. "We didn't take everything to your grandparents' house."

My mouth dropped open. "Really?" I said.

"Maybe if you open yours you will find something for the party."

"Oh, Mom. You're the greatest!" I rushed to the tree. Sure enough, there were four wrapped packages with my name on the tags. Inside the boxes were cute outfits from The Gap, Old Navy, Express, and Eddie Bauer. This was going to be a great new year.

"Laurel, I don't want to go to a party," Foster said as we played Scrabble in my den that night. "I want to be in church."

"We will go to church," I assured him. "We'll just leave there a little early and go to Brittany's party."

"Brittany is not someone I want to hang out with," he said, absentmindedly playing with his letter tiles. "I want to spend that night thanking God for what He's done for me this year and for what He's going to bless me with next year. Why do you want to go to a party when you could be doing that?"

I was sick of questions, and it was obvious that this was going nowhere. "Fine," I said with a sigh. "I guess you and I will just do different things on New Year's Eve."

"What?" he said. "But you said you'd go to church with me."

"I will," I said. "But then I'm going to Brittany's party."

As promised, I attended church with Foster on New Year's Eve. Then, at ten o'clock, Meagan came by to take me to Brittany's house.

When I walked in the door, I saw kids and beer bottles everywhere. I also saw a big brass bell hanging from the ceiling in the entryway. But I did not see Brittany's parents.

OK, Lord, I just made another wrong decision. I left a peaceful candlelight service with my family and my boyfriend to come to a crazy party packed with drunk teenagers.

"Hey, Laurel!" Brittany screamed over the music as soon as she saw me. She pulled me into the kitchen. "I'm so glad you came."

"Where are your parents?" I screamed back.

"They had to go out of town," she hollered into my ear. "Stop being so uptight. Here," she said, shoving a cup full of punch into my hands. "Drink this." I was really thirsty, so I took a big gulp. "Whoa, don't drink it so fast," Brittany cautioned. "You're gonna get sick."

"Sick?" I asked. Then I noticed a bitter aftertaste. "What's in here? Is this stuff spiked?"

"I just wanted you to have a good time," she said, laughing.

I wanted to be angry, but I suddenly felt light and care-free. The punch was delicious. I took another sip.

A guy from school grabbed my hand and pulled me into the living room. A bunch of kids were trying to dance in the space between the couches and chairs that had been pushed against the walls. It was crowded, but I didn't care. I threw my hands in the air and started shaking my body. I was having a blast, but after an hour or so I started feeling dizzy. I was about to fall, so I wrapped my arms around the guy's neck to keep myself upright.

Suddenly, over the music, everyone started counting. "Ten! Nine! Eight!" I felt the guy's hands settle on my behind. I wanted to move them but I couldn't release my hold on the guy's neck without falling to the floor.

I glanced around the room. It started spinning. The crowd yelled, "Three!" I saw someone who looked like Foster standing just inside the doorway on the far side of the room. I tried to pry myself away from the guy with his hands on my behind, but as I did, the crowd screamed, "One!" The guy kissed me. His mouth tasted like alcohol, and he slobbered all over me.

Brittany screamed out, "Happy New Year!" and started ringing the bell.

standing
for Christ

"Laurel, are you OK?" Meagan asked after I pulled myself away from the sloppy kisser. "You look like you're about to fall down." She pointed to the cup in my hand. "Did you drink some of this?"

"Just a sip," I said, my head still foggy. "I think. Maybe a couple of sips. I really don't remember. Where did Foster go?"

"Foster was here?" she asked, looking around.

"Yeah, I just saw him at the door. I've got to go find him."

With my heart racing, I looked everywhere for my boyfriend. Suddenly, someone grabbed my arm and twirled me around.

"Hey, where are you going?" Branson said, still clutching my elbow. "Let's dance in the new year." My ex-boyfriend wrapped his arms around my waist and started twisting my body.

"Stop it," I begged. "You're making me dizzy!"

He stopped and looked into my eyes. "Laurel, have you been drinking?" He grinned. "Now I know we're gonna dance the night away! It's about time you decided to loosen up." He picked up a paper cup from the buffet table. "Here, have another drink." He placed the red cup against my lips and tilted. Some of the punch spilled onto my cream sweater, but most of it went down my throat.

"What's in this stuff?" I asked, trying not to choke.

"Not like you'd know if I told you, but it's a combination of rum, vodka, and Scotch. And a tiny bit of fruit punch."

"It's nasty." I took a sniff of the concoction and crinkled my nose.

"Come on, babe," he said, slipping his arm around me again. "Let's dance. I'll have Bo put on a special song for us."

"I've got a headache," I said. It was true. I was starting to lose my balance. The room was spinning around. I felt sick to my stomach.

"Tell me the truth, Laurel," he said, putting his lips close to my ear so he wouldn't have to yell the words. "You were jealous when you saw me with Brittany. Admit it."

His words caused some of the haze in my brain to clear. "No, Branson," I said carefully. "I'm sorry, but you are dead wrong. I don't need you in my life to be happy. And I'm not jealous. I have God. He's the one who makes me happy. And He has given me Foster."

Branson leered at me. "Oh yeah? Well, where is that fine, righteous boy now? In church somewhere? With your dad? While you're here drinking? Laurel, you may love God, but you're just like the rest of us."

"I am not," I cried. I didn't want to be like these people.

Branson stroked my hair. "It's OK, Laurel. Alcohol isn't going to kill you. You might as well get used to it, because that's what college is all about. You'd look pretty stupid if you got there and couldn't hold your liquor."

I pushed him out of my way and headed for the hallway.

"Wait," he called after me. "I want my New Year's kiss."

I ignored him and started searching the rooms. I still couldn't find Foster, so I headed for the front door.

"You'll be back," Branson yelled as I dashed out into the cold night.

It had been so crowded in Brittany's house, the fresh air felt wonderful. I noticed some movement down the street. When I looked more carefully, I recognized Foster getting into his midnight blue Toyota Celica. I started skipping down the steps, suddenly realizing I was still holding the cup of punch.

"Wait," I called out. "Foster, don't go!"

Either he didn't hear me or he didn't care what I had to say, because he got into his car without hesitation. He started to drive up the street. I stood in the middle of the road to stop him.

Foster slammed on his brakes, then got out of the car. "Laurel, what's wrong with you?" he asked in a panicked voice. "What are you doing in the middle of the street?"

"I was trying to catch you," I said. "I wanted to wish you a happy New Year!" I started to swing my arms around his neck but spilled my punch all over his coat.

He jumped back. "I gotta go," he said, and he swung back around toward his car.

"Wait," I begged, grabbing his arm. "I don't feel good. Please don't leave me. I need you."

"I told you not to come to this party," he said, looking straight into my eyes. "I knew something would go wrong."

"I'm sorry," I whimpered. "I just wanted something to drink. I didn't know there was alcohol in the punch. Then, as I started to loosen up, it began to taste pretty good."

"I thought you were stronger than this," he said.

"Why are you putting me down? It was a mistake. It's no big deal."

"You're right." He broke free of my grasp. "Since it's no

big deal, why don't you just go back to the party and let your friends take care of you!"

Foster got back in the car, pulled around me, and drove away. I was devastated. I took another sip of my punch and went back inside. I desperately needed to sit down. As I wandered around looking for an empty chair, Kirsten Wells confronted me.

"Well, looky here," my brunette teammate from Rockdale County Gym said, placing a hand on her petite waist. "If it isn't Laurel Shadrach. The one who acts perfect for Coach Milligent just so she can try to make the rest of us look bad."

"Hey, I never try to outdo anyone but myself," I replied to Miss Uppity. She rolled her coppery green eyes at me. "Believe what you want, I'm tired of trying to defend my ability."

She peered at my paper cup and raised an eyebrow. "And now you're drinking hard liquor. What a hypocrite! I wish Coach could see you right now."

I used the loud music as an excuse to raise my voice. "I never said I was perfect, even though you say it all the time. Well, now you see that I'm not. So just get off my back." I brushed past her to continue my search for a place to sit. Not finding one, I finally sat on the floor against the wall and put the cup down beside me.

Don't you feel just horrible? I heard my conscience say.

No, my flesh battled back.

You should, my heart persisted. *Sure, Kirsten seems all relaxed and cool on the outside. But remember what you overheard at that last practice before Christmas break? She lost her boyfriend. Again.*

"Laurel?"

I looked up and saw my boyfriend standing over me. "Foster," I whimpered. "I thought you left."

"I did. But then I realized that you really need me to be here, even though I don't approve of your drinking."

My stomach churned. "I really feel sick," I groaned.

Foster helped me to the bathroom. Within seconds I was throwing up.

After regaining some composure, I came out of the bathroom. Foster was waiting in the hallway just outside the door. "Thanks for coming back," I said. "It really is sweet of you to care so much about me."

He gave me a sad smile. "You know I care, Laurel. I was angry, but I shouldn't have left."

I melted into his arms. "Let's just say I won't be doing this again. I don't understand how people can get a thrill out of alcohol. My head really hurts!"

"Probably because you drank too fast," he said. "Let's get you some water, then go outside for a little fresh air."

Foster led me slowly down the hall to the kitchen, where he poured me a tall glass of water. I took a sip then let him escort me outside. I sat on the porch swing, and Foster sat close beside me.

"You're going to feel pretty bad tomorrow," he said, curling his arm around my shoulders.

I groaned. "I've already learned my lesson."

"What a great girlfriend I have," he said, smiling. "She learns so fast."

I hugged him tightly and gave him a grin. "Happy New Year."

He laughed. "Hearing that you've learned your lesson tells me this might be a happy new year after all."

With the little energy I had left, I chuckled at Foster's humor. In the midst of my craziness, God had sent him to rescue me. Although I didn't have all of my faculties, I was thankful from the depths of my soul.

People started coming out of the house and heading for home. Some climbed into taxis, obviously too drunk to drive. Several others started sauntering down the sidewalk, although most of them couldn't keep a straight line. I was surprised at how many climbed behind the wheels of their cars and drove off, either with tires screeching or so slow they were barely moving.

"I sure hope they all get home OK," I said. "We should pray about that."

"Yes, we should," Foster agreed. We whispered a quick prayer for the safety of everyone who had been at the party.

"We've got to get you cleaned up before I take you home," he said after the amen.

"I'm going to crash here," I said. "I told my parents I wouldn't be home till tomorrow."

Foster and I said good night at his car, then I walked slowly up to Brittany's room. I still felt horrible—spiritually and physically. Mentally, I was starting to get a grip. As I drifted off to sleep, I promised myself and God that I would stick to my commitment and never do anything like this again.

"Laurel, wake up!" I heard Brittany and Meagan say.

I didn't know how much time had passed, but waking up was not the thing I wanted to do.

"Laurel, it's your brother Lance," Meagan said.

I forced my eyes to open. "What about him?" I asked, trying to focus.

"He came to my party," Brittany whined, "and now he's drunk. Passed out in the downstairs bathroom!"

I groaned, wishing I could go back to sleep. "What time is it?" I asked, my voice groggy.

"It's three in the morning," Brittany informed me, sounding both irritated and panicked.

"He's got to go home," Meagan said. "Your parents are probably worried sick about him."

"But he's not sober enough to drive," Brittany added.

"He can't drive anyway," I said, sitting up in Brittany's bed and holding my throbbing head. "He doesn't have his license."

"Then how did he get here?"

"I saw your mom's van in the driveway," Meagan announced.

"What?" I squealed. "He stole Mom's van?"

Brittany shrugged. "I guess."

"I've got to see him." I crawled out of the bed, my legs feeling like overcooked linguini.

Meagan and Brittany followed me down to the basement. Lance sat on the bathroom floor beside the toilet, saying all kinds of stuff but not making any sense.

"You've got to call someone," Brittany whispered, not taking her frightened eyes off my brother. "If your parents send the police out looking for him and they find him here, I could get in a lot of trouble."

"I can't call my parents," I moaned. "What would I tell them?"

"I don't know," Meagan said, shaking her head as she looked at Lance.

I couldn't imagine my brother stealing the family van, but that was the only thing that made sense. I had stepped in and saved him before, but I couldn't do it again.

Then again, was that any way to act toward my brother? I had made the drinking mistake myself, and if it wasn't for Foster, who knows how I would have ended up? Maybe my brother deserved a little more grace.

"I've gotta drive him home," I said.

Brittany gasped. "I thought you were gonna stay and help me clean up. This place is a mess! I can't take care of this all by myself."

"I've got to get my brother home, Brittany," I repeated. "There's no other way."

"Do you feel OK to drive?" Meagan asked.

"Yeah," I said. "I'll be all right . . . I hope."

"You need some coffee," Brittany decided. "There's some upstairs."

"What's coffee gonna do?" I asked, watching her traipse up the steps.

"Wake you up," she replied over her shoulder.

I stared at my brother, who had passed out again. "I can get him into the car if you guys both help me," I said to Meagan. "But once I get home, I don't know how I'm gonna get him up to his room. I don't want to get caught. My parents would be so disappointed in both of us."

"We'll have to get him some coffee, too, then," Meagan said.

"Good idea."

As we walked upstairs to the kitchen, Meagan asked, "How are you going to explain to your parents why you didn't spend the night here after all?"

"I don't know," I said, unable to think clearly through the fog in my brain.

After thirty minutes of pouring coffee into my brother's mouth, I got him somewhat coherent. With my girlfriends' help, I piled him into the van and headed toward home.

I glanced at his slumped body leaning against the car door, his eyes closed. "Lance, I don't know if you can hear me or not, but this is ridiculous. How could you steal Mom's van?"

"Steal?" he said, his speech slurred. "I'm part of this family, and this is a family car. I was gonna have it back by morning."

As I pulled into the driveway we came up with a game plan. We would go into the house through the back door, and Lance would sleep on the couch. Since he shared a bedroom with Liam and Luke, we couldn't risk getting him up to his bed. In the morning, he would tell our parents that he fell asleep watching the ball drop in Times Square on TV. After helping him to the couch, I would go back outside, walk around to the front door, then go up to my room. If my parents saw me, I would say that Brittany's mom had dropped me off.

I got my brother through the back OK, but as I came back in through the front door, Liam, my oldest younger brother, suddenly appeared out of the darkness.

"You scared me!" I yelled at him in a whisper.

"Laurel, what's going on?" he asked, peering at me.

"What are you talking about?" I asked.

"I saw you driving Mom's van," he said. "Where's Lance?"

I rolled my eyes. "Why do you have to know everything?"

"Why do you have to hide things?" he countered.

"Aren't you supposed to be asleep?" I argued, starting to walk away.

Liam grabbed my arm. "I was asleep. Until Meagan called."

I stopped and looked up at him. "Did Mom and Dad wake up?"

"No," he said. "She called my private line."

"Did she tell you what's going on with Lance?" I asked.

He nodded. "I can't believe you're gonna cover for him. And Meagan told me you said this wasn't the first time."

"Well, Meagan's got a big mouth," I said, yanking my arm out of his grasp and storming toward the stairs.

"Laurel, don't walk away from me. We need to talk about this."

I turned around. "Liam, if you want to talk about this, then talk about it with Lance in the morning."

"Laurel, if Lance has a problem with alcohol, you're not helping him by covering it up. You're just making it worse."

Hearing him speak the words my mind had been torturing me with only made me more irritated. "Good night," I said, then hurried upstairs before he could say anything more.

———————

A few hours later, my mom opened my bedroom door. "Laurel," she said, "I thought you were spending the night at Brittany's. Are you all right? When did you come home?"

"I got in early this morning," I said groggily. "I have gymnastics this afternoon, so I need to get some more sleep."

"On New Year's Day?" Mom asked. "That doesn't seem right."

I rolled over and buried myself deeper into the covers. "It's the first practice with the new school team," I explained, moaning. "We want to go to nationals, and top athletes don't take breaks."

"OK, honey," Mom said. As she closed my bedroom door, she added, "Happy New Year."

Later that morning I awoke to the sound of two of my brothers fighting. I figured from their noise level that they had to be the only ones in the house. Unable to sleep through the racket, I crawled out of bed, slipped into my robe, and ventured into the hallway. The noise was coming from the boys' bedroom. I wandered down the hall and peeked around the open door. "Do you two mind?" I groaned. "I have a headache."

"Laurel, stay out of this," Liam said.

"Don't get on her case," Lance replied. "She was helping me out."

"You need to watch it," Liam threatened, "or I'll tell Mom and Dad about your drinking binge."

"Hey, I'm not gonna let you hold this over my head forever. If you're going to tell, then tell. Let them come down on me. You're not my parent." Lance brushed past me and left the room.

Liam turned on me next. "So you think you're helping him out by keeping this a secret? You're hurting him worse than you know."

"Yeah, yeah." I shook my head, but only slightly since it hurt so much. "You told me that last night. Unless you have something new to say, I've got to get to practice." Without waiting for an answer, I walked out of the room.

————————

After my head started to clear, feelings of guilt crept into my mind. All during gymnastics practice at the school, I kept slipping off the bars because I couldn't concentrate. What if Liam was right? Had I made things worse for Lance by keeping my mouth shut? I knew I shouldn't be making up stories and lying to my folks.

I attempted a simple maneuver on the balance beam, my favorite piece of equipment and the area I excelled at most. But I felt so frustrated, I blew my approach. After hitting the beam with my fist, I shed a tear.

All the girls stared at me. I didn't recognize any of them, and I wondered if they knew I was going to be the team captain. The captain was supposed to be the best. Instead, I looked like the worst.

"Laurel," my coach called out, "can you come here a second?"

I went into Mrs. Turner's office and took a seat.

"Is there something going on that I'm not aware of?" she probed, closing the glass door.

"No." I fidgeted in my seat. "I just stayed up a little late last night. You know, for New Year's Eve."

"I'm beginning to regret asking you to come to practice today. Coach Milligent told me you'd learned a new routine. He said you could perform it for us at our first meet. Do I need to hold off on putting you in?"

"No," I assured her quickly. I knew when Mrs. Turner offered to make me captain of the school team that my practices with Coach Milligent at the county gym would take a backseat. But I also felt the two teams might complement each other. I didn't want to lose the respect of either of my coaches. "I was just a little off track," I said. "Things will be better tomorrow."

"Well, why don't you go on home now and come back tomorrow, then?"

I went straight to the locker room to change into street clothes. As I was getting ready to leave, I heard two of the girls on our team come in and start talking on the other side of my row of lockers.

"He's a senior, and he's got brown hair," one said in a babyish voice. She giggled. "He is so cute!"

"Have you talked to him?" the other asked.

She giggled again. "No."

"You've got to be aggressive, girl."

I must have still had some alcohol in my system, because I stuck my nose in where it didn't belong. "Never let a guy know you like him," I said, coming around the corner of the lockers. "That really turns guys off. You've got to have some dignity about yourselves." The girls stared at me. "What are your names?" I asked.

"I'm Shaney," one of the girls said. I recognized her voice as the one who liked this boy. Shaney was cute and blonde, with a petite figure.

"My name is Madison," said her friend.

"I'm Laurel," I said.

"Oh, we know who you are," Shaney said. "We're so excited you're on the team. You're so good!"

I felt my cheeks redden. "Well, my practice today didn't show it."

"We all have bad days," Madison replied. "Don't worry about it."

"Thanks," I said.

"Isn't Lance Shadrach your brother?" Shaney asked.

"Yeah." So they did know some things about me.

"How is he?" she asked shyly.

I could tell she liked him, but I wasn't going to set Lance up with anyone until he got himself together. "He's . . . sick right now," I told her.

She looked sad. "I hope he gets better."

"Yeah, me too."

———————————

Two weeks passed. My practices got much better after that first day. Foster and I were doing well too. We were studying the Word and praying together often.

But I didn't talk to Lance at all. It felt like he was avoiding me. I prayed for him every day.

"Lord," I whispered beside my bed one morning, "please forgive me for drinking on New Year's Eve. I know that being drunk is a sin, and I don't want to sin against You. I should have stayed at church on New Year's Eve. Thank You for helping me to regain my focus on gymnastics. Lord, Lance seems so distant lately. Please reach him, Lord. Help him know that You love him. Thank You for loving me and forgiving me."

As Foster and I walked through the hall at school that day, we talked about the New Year's Eve party at Brittany's. "I still wonder why I had a desire to taste that alcohol," I said.

"It's easy to do the wrong thing when we're tempted to do something we've never tried before," he observed. "The key is not doing it again."

"You're right," I said. "I've definitely learned my lesson."

The bell was about to ring, so we went our separate ways. I headed for choir, which I had with Robyn, a black girl I'd met in chemistry class on the first day of school. I was looking forward to chatting with my new friend. Unfortunately, by the time I got to class, our choir director, Mrs. Moreland, had already started.

After class Robyn came up to me. "Hey," she said, "Monday is Martin Luther King Jr. Day. Do you have any plans?"

"My church is having a special service in the morning, and in the afternoon we're supposed to feed the homeless," I said. "Why?"

"There's a celebration at the King Center and my mom is selling books there. They need some hostesses. She told me to ask if you wanted to help. You could come by in the evening, after you're done with your church thing."

"That'd be great," I said. I was always thrilled to help Robyn's mom. It felt great to know a real author, especially one who wrote novels for teens. I hoped she might ask me to look over another manuscript for her.

Saturday afternoon, after gymnastics practice at Rockdale County Gym, I had a three-way call with Brittany and Meagan. I told them about my plans for Martin Luther King Jr. Day.

"I don't understand why you have to go anywhere with that Robyn girl instead of hanging out with us," Brittany whined.

"She already told you," Meagan said. "She's going to volunteer. We can do something together later."

Brittany huffed. "It's not even a real holiday."

"It's a holiday," I defended. "If it wasn't for Dr. King, no minorities would be able to vote. I appreciate what he did. He stood for something." I got nothing but silence on the phone line. "So, what are you guys going to do for the holiday?"

"I'm not celebrating it at all," Brittany said.

That Monday night, as I performed my duties as hostess at the King Center, I felt uneasy. Something was wrong with me, but I couldn't tell what it was. As I greeted visitors, I thought about the life of Martin Luther King Jr. Then I thought about my own life.

What did I stand for? What did I truly believe in? Sure, I was a Christian. I had accepted Jesus Christ as my Lord and Savior years ago. But was I doing everything God had called me to do? Could people around me see Christ in me? Was I willing to give up my so-called rights, possibly even risk death, so that God could use my life to bring honor to Himself?

"What's wrong, Laurel?" Robyn asked, interrupting my thoughts. "You look upset."

No visitors were approaching, so I opened up to her. "I'm disappointed in myself," I said. "I want my passion for Christ to burn strong. But lately, I've been giving in to temptation. I don't want that any longer. I want to be standing for Christ."

betting
on games

hat's my phone!" Brittany exclaimed. Keeping both hands on the steering wheel, she hollered, "Answer it, Laurel!"

It had been a long day. I had forty minutes between school and gymnastics practice, and Brittany was running me up to Chik-Fil-A to get a snack. I hated relying on Brittany for rides everywhere, but it did give us a chance to hang out a lot together.

I looked around the car for her phone but couldn't locate it. "Where is it?" I uttered in frustration.

"In the glove compartment," she said. "I forgot to put it in my purse this morning." I twisted the knob on the glove box. "It's probably someone calling me about my dinner plans," Brittany moaned. "I wonder if it's Jeff or Chris."

"Who are Jeff and Chris?" I asked, pulling the ringing phone out of the compartment.

"Some guys I met at my party," she said. "They go to

Rockdale High." She peered into the caller ID window. "I don't recognize this number. I bet it's that guy from Heritage High." She punched a button and put the phone to her ear. "Hello?" she said in a seductive voice.

With a sudden change in her tone, she grumbled, "Yeah, it's me. Yes, I'll be in. I know it's important. No, I don't have another number where you can reach me." She sighed. "Look, stop calling me, OK? I said I was coming in."

She closed the phone hard then put her head on the wheel. Since her foot was still on the gas, the car started swerving to the wrong side of the road.

"Brittany, what are you doing?" I shrieked.

"Oh!" She lifted her head and maneuvered back onto the right side of the road.

What was all that about? I wondered. Then it dawned on me. I had been so wrapped up in getting back into school after the holidays, I hadn't really thought about Brittany's trip to the doctor. She'd gone in shortly before the Christmas break, after she heard that an old boyfriend had contracted AIDS. It hadn't been easy convincing her to get herself tested.

"You haven't gone to get the test results yet, have you?" I questioned her. She stared at the road in silence. "Brittany, this is important. AIDS is nothing to play around with."

Brittany shot me an angry glare. "Don't you think I know that?"

"If you know, then why are you putting off getting those results?"

She took a deep breath. "When I took the test," she said quietly, "I was 90 percent sure I was OK. But when the clinic called me a few days later, they refused to give me the results over the phone. Said I had to come in to get them." Her hands started shaking on the steering wheel. "I figured that if I was OK the clinic wouldn't call me back. But they did. And they just keep calling. I know they want me to come in, but . . . I'm scared."

The car started drifting out of its lane again as Brittany's eyes filled with tears. I reached over and grabbed the wheel. My friend relaxed her gas-pedal foot and the car slowed down. I guided the car to the curb and then put it in park. Brittany laid her head on the steering wheel and sobbed.

"You don't need to drive," I assured her. "Just sit here for a while. Once you get yourself together, you can go to the clinic."

"I can't, Laurel," she wailed.

"Britt, if there's something wrong, don't you want to know?"

She lifted her head and turned to me, her face drenched with tears and her eyes wide with fright. "Laurel, why are you talking like that?" Her voice quivered. "You think something's wrong, don't you? If I was OK the lady would stop calling, right?" I'd never heard my friend's voice so filled with fear.

"Maybe that's just procedure," I said, trying to assure her. "Don't get all worked up about it. Just go. You need to know."

"I wish I was a virgin like you," she said. "Then I wouldn't have to go through this mess."

In my mind I said a quick prayer that my next words would be filled with God's wisdom. Only He would know the right thing to say at this moment. Thankfully, something came to my mind that I'd learned in a Bible study at church. "It's not easy walking backward, Brittany," I said, "but it can be done. Ask God to forgive you, and then walk away from your sin. That's called repentance." I prayed that my words would reach her heart, not just her ears. The look in her eyes told me she had heard the message, but wasn't able to respond yet, at least not in words. "Now," I said, not wanting to miss the opportunity, "are you ready to get those test results?"

"Laurel, I'm scared. What if it's bad news? I could die."

"You'll cross that road when you get to it," I said. "If you get to it."

"Will you come with me?" she asked.

"I wish I could," I said sincerely. "But I've got gymnastics practice."

"We don't have to go now. We can go whenever it's convenient for you."

I knew she was just trying to get out of it. "Come on, Brittany. You can do this."

Her sad face grew hard. "Fine," she said, wiping her tears. "Just go to gymnastics. I'll do this on my own." She put the car into drive, pulled away from the curb, and continued on toward the school.

She was lashing out at me. But I understood why, so I didn't take it personally. Her problems at that moment were bigger than mine, so I didn't need to add to them by being angry with her.

I asked if she'd let me pray with her, but she said she wasn't in the mood. I promised I would continue praying for her anyway. "The Lord doesn't want to be closed off in times of trouble," I told her. "That's when He wants us to open our hearts and arms and totally let Him in to fix it all."

"I don't believe this," I said as I walked into the empty school gym.

My life was getting too full and complicated. Being on two gymnastics teams was turning out to be more difficult than I'd thought it would be. School practices were on Monday and Wednesday afternoons. I was supposed to practice at Rockdale County Gym on Tuesdays and Thursdays. Today was Tuesday. *I guess the Monday holiday messed me up.*

Not having a car was getting old. My eighteenth birthday was in six months, and the only thing I wanted was four wheels. I didn't need a flashy new Jetta like Brittany's. Anything reliable would satisfy me.

As I walked to the office to use the phone, I wondered who I could call to pick me up and take me all the way across town to the county gym. I quickly crossed several people off my list, including my parents. I didn't want to hear them tell me how irresponsible I was. I also crossed off Coach Milligent, who would yell at me for being absent-minded. Besides, he'd already started the practice, and I didn't want to pull him away from the other girls. Meagan was horseback riding, so I couldn't call her. I thought about Robyn, but we hadn't been friends for very long and I didn't want to seem like I was using her. I decided to call Brittany.

"Hello?" she answered the phone.

"Hey, Britt, it's me."

"OK, I'm going," she grumbled. "You don't have to check up on me. I'll leave in a second."

I looked out the office window and saw Brittany's car, still parked in the lot. "You're still here?"

"Yeah," she said meekly. "Why aren't you practicing?"

"I need to take another ride with you," I said.

"Oh, thank you, Laurel! Thank you! I knew you were my friend."

Her excitement confused me, but I grabbed my stuff and rushed outside. At least, since she was still there, it would save me some time getting to practice.

When I busted out the front door of the school gym, I saw Brittany standing near the passenger side of the car, holding the door open for me. That was totally unlike her.

"Thanks," I said, sliding in.

"We'd better hurry," she said as she dropped into the driver's seat and cranked up the car.

"Yeah, you're not kidding," I replied.

When Brittany started driving in the opposite direction of the gym, I realized she was not taking me where I wanted to go. It suddenly dawned on me that she was heading for the clinic. I was so happy she was going that I wasn't about to tell her I couldn't go with her. Something deep within told me that nothing was more important than being with a friend who needed me.

When Brittany pulled into the clinic parking lot, she

stared at it like it was the enemy. I grabbed her hand, which was tightly gripped around the steering wheel, and started praying.

"Father," I said, "we thank You that You are in control of all things. We thank You, also, Lord, that You stand ready to forgive us when we come to You in repentance. Brittany is in a tough position right now, so I ask that You have mercy on her and give her the courage to go in there and get those results."

I paused. I had so much more to say. God had to hear my every word. This was important.

I continued praying. "I know You promise Your children that You will cause all things to work together for their good, even bad things. So I pray You will help Brittany to trust You and give her life to You. She doesn't have to go through this alone. I thank You that You brought us together so I can be here for her. And I thank You that no matter what the results, You stand waiting for her with open arms. In Jesus' name we pray, amen."

"Thank you," Brittany said. "I needed that."

"Are you ready to go in?" I asked gently.

"Not quite yet. Can we just sit here for a second?"

"Sure," I said. "Whenever you're ready we'll go."

After about five minutes, Brittany got out of the car. We walked hand in hand into the clinic.

Why is this taking so long? I had been sitting in the lobby waiting for Brittany for twenty-five minutes.

I stared at the phone on the receptionist's desk. I wanted to call the gym, but what would I say? Finally, I walked up to the nurse. "Hi," I said, getting her attention. "Could you please tell my friend Brittany Cox that I have to go?"

"Sure," she said kindly. "I'll be right back."

I stood at the receptionist's desk for several minutes, trying not to tap my feet. But instead of the receptionist, the doctor came out. The look on his face made my heart fall to the ground. I knew Brittany had not received good news.

"Can you please come back for a moment?" he asked quietly.

I put my hand to my mouth and tears started filling my eyes as I followed the doctor to a back room. After gently closing the door, he confirmed my worst fears. "Your friend tested positive for HIV. When we told her the results, she started crying uncontrollably. She was so overcome, we had to sedate her. She should be coming around soon. Her mother is on the way, but in the meantime, she's going to need a friend. Can you come with me, please."

Having sex before marriage is such a gamble, I thought as I followed the doctor down a long hallway. *There are so many risks.* Brittany had given everything to that guy she had sex with. Not just her body, but her life. I knew God designed sex to be cherished and enjoyed in the marriage relationship and no other. When we ignore His design we pay the price. But why did it have to be this way for Brittany?

Earlier that year, my friend Robyn had spun the sex wheel and it landed on pregnancy. Just like alcohol was for my grandfather, sex was addictive for Brittany. She had spun the wheel one too many times.

I looked at Brittany, who was sitting on a hospital bed, rolled up in a ball, rocking back and forth in agony.

Lord, I know she didn't abide by Your rules. But did it have to be this bad?

I hurried over to her and tried to stop the rocking by holding her in my arms.

"I have AIDS, Laurel," she sobbed, clutching me tightly. "Why, Laurel? Why? This isn't fair."

"No, it's not," I whispered. "But it will be OK."

"How?" she shrieked. "How will it be OK? And don't give me any of your Christian platitudes. I don't believe in God anymore."

I gasped. "Britt, don't say that. You gave your life to Him. Don't flip-flop."

I felt her body stiffen. "I can take it back if I want. I'm going to die, Laurel."

The doctor, who had been standing behind me, came closer and looked kindly at Brittany. "That's not quite true, young lady." We both looked at him. "You became hysterical before we could discuss your situation." He indicated a chair for me, and I sat beside Brittany's bed.

"To begin with, just because someone is HIV positive, that doesn't automatically mean that he or she has AIDS. HIV and AIDS are not the same."

"They're not?" we both asked at the same time.

"A person who is HIV positive can live for a long time and may not even feel sick for many years."

"What's going to happen to her, Doctor?" I asked.

"Every individual case is unique," he explained. "But generally, as the HIV disease continues, it slowly wears down the immune system. Then viruses, parasites, fungi, and bacteria that usually don't cause any problems can make the infected person quite ill. Once HIV has weakened the immune system over several years, the body becomes open to invasion and attacks from other diseases. This is what can lead to getting AIDS."

I wasn't sure I understood everything the doctor was saying. But I did catch two things. I rejoiced in the news that my friend could still live for many years. But I could see a lifetime of deterioration in her health, and that frightened me. I could only begin to imagine how it must be affecting her.

"We caught this at an early stage," the doctor continued, "so we can treat it. We can't cure it, but we can treat it."

Brittany was staring at the doctor in stunned silence, obviously unable to speak, probably unable to comprehend everything he was saying. But I wanted to get whatever information I could. "What treatments are available?" I asked.

"There is a drug called Viracept that can be taken in combination with other HIV drugs." He pulled a small pad of paper from his lab coat pocket and scribbled on the top

50

sheet. "She should take five pills twice a day. Each pill is 250 milligrams."

Brittany started to look calmer. Maybe she'd been listening after all. The doctor tore off the prescription and handed it to Brittany. Just then, Mr. and Mrs. Cox came in.

"You called my parents?" Brittany screamed when she saw them.

Mr. Cox stood a few feet away from the bed and stared at Brittany. "I knew she had too much time on her hands," he said coldly.

"Too much time on her hands?" Mrs. Cox repeated, glaring at her husband. "She's involved in everything! Cheerleading, modeling, beauty pageants. She's always busy doing things."

"Yeah, but who was monitoring her?" Mr. Cox said, his arms crossed tightly over his chest. "Did you know she was sleeping around?"

"Did you know she was?" Mrs. Cox shot back.

Brittany slid off the bed, her face red. "This is why I never tell you guys anything!" Her voice sounded brittle. "You're always arguing. I can't deal with you right now." She grabbed her small black purse and ran out of the room.

"Where does she think she's going?" Mr. Cox asked.

"You pushed her away, like always," his wife yelled back.

The doctor cleared his throat. "We do need to talk with her," he said.

"I'll get her." I asked Brittany's mother if she could call my mom and explain to her where I was. She thanked me for being there for Brittany and assured me that she would call my parents.

I found Brittany sitting in her car, crying. I stood at the driver's side window and tried to talk her into coming back inside.

"No way," she said, her eyes red-rimmed and brimming with tears. "Either get in now, or I'll leave you in the parking lot and not come back."

Her words reminded me of the night Branson had done just that. He'd tried to convince me to give it up for him, and when I said no, he drove away. I had to hitch a ride home, after curfew, from Jackson Reid, Robyn's date, who had been getting it on with her in his car a few yards away.

I jumped into Brittany's Jetta. As she sped through the parking lot, I realized I wasn't equipped to deal with this at all.

"Britt, slow down, OK?" I said as her tires screeched around a curve in the road. She ran a red light.

I clutched the door handle and pressed my feet against the floorboards. She wasn't just jeopardizing her own life and health, but mine and others on the road as well.

Finally, she pulled into her driveway. "Oh," she said, "I've got to take you home."

"No, that's OK," I said. "I'll just go inside with you and call my parents."

"No, I want to take you home," she insisted. "Just hold on here a second, I'll be right back." She got out of the car and hurried into her house. She came out carrying a small brown paper bag. Without a word, Brittany pulled back out of her driveway and sped down the street. When she'd driven past her neighborhood, she reached into the bag, twisted something inside it, then lifted it to her lips. As she started drinking out of the bag, a bitter smell reached my nostrils.

"What are you doing?" I shrieked.

"What does it look like?" she said, wiping her lips and sticking the bag between her legs. "I'm drinking a beer."

"Are you crazy? Alcohol will only make things worse!"

Brittany shrugged. "Laurel, what's it gonna hurt, huh? I'm HIV positive. It's all downhill from here, anyway."

"C'mon, Britt."

"What?" she said, a sharp edge in her voice. "You want some?" She picked up the bag and held it out toward me.

"Yeah," I said. I reached out but she snatched it back. Some of the beer spilled on my lap.

"Oh man, Brittany!" I cried out, trying to brush it off with my hands.

"Maybe I should drink some down so it doesn't spill again." She took a big gulp.

"Brittany, why are you playing games with me?"

"Wait," she teased. "I bet you can catch it this time. Let me just drink some more." She took another swig, then put the bottle down quickly as she maneuvered another corner.

"Brittany, this isn't funny, and it isn't safe. Why are you doing this to yourself?"

Without answering, she just started driving faster. Her recklessness was really scaring me. All of a sudden, blue lights started flashing behind us.

"Oh, that's great," Brittany groaned. "He actually thinks I'm going to pull over."

I couldn't believe what I was hearing. "Britt, that's the police. Stop the car!"

She grinned. "Let's have a little fun. Cheer me on, Laurel. You always said you wanted to be a cheerleader." She gunned the engine.

"Brittany, stop!"

Sirens blared behind us, and a stern voice over a loudspeaker demanded that we pull over immediately.

"Oh, OK." Brittany sighed, slowing the car. "Whatever." She handed me the bag and told me to put it under my seat. When I took it, it felt light. I peeked inside and noticed the bottle was nearly empty. I stuffed it under my seat.

Brittany used one hand to turn the wheel toward the curb, and the other to grab a piece of gum out of her purse. She unwrapped it and started smacking.

"Hand me my registration from the glove compartment," she said. Then she rolled down her window and gave the policeman a big, sweet smile. "Officer," she asked in an innocent voice, "was I doing something wrong?" She batted her eyes at the young uniformed man.

He didn't smile back. "Ma'am, why did you drive faster when I signaled you over?"

"I thought you'd enjoy the chase," she said with a giggle. "I wanted to make you work a little to get me. See, that's what's wrong with you men. You think girls are easy."

The policeman asked for her driver's license and registration.

"What are you going to do?" Brittany asked boldly as she handed him her papers. "Take me to jail? Whoop-de-do! My life is over anyway. If I'm in jail, the taxpayers can pay for my medical bills." She lowered her head to the steering wheel and started weeping.

The young policeman blinked and looked over at me.

"I'm sorry, officer," I said. "My friend just got some devastating news and she isn't thinking rationally."

"Oh, really?" His eyebrows raised, as if he'd heard that excuse a million times.

"Yes sir," I said. I didn't want to tell my friend's business, but I didn't want her hauled off to jail, either. I lowered my voice, even though no one was around to hear. "She just got the results of an HIV test."

"Oh." He looked surprised, then seriously concerned. Brittany didn't look up, but her sobbing lessened, and I knew she was listening.

"I can drive her home," I offered.

He studied both of us for a moment. "I don't usually let teenagers go, but I'll make an exception this time as long as you promise to get your friend home safely."

"Oh, I will, officer," I promised, getting out of the car.

He waited for Brittany to climb out of the driver's seat and for me to take her place. Then he handed me Brittany's license and registration. "You girls have a safe day."

As the policeman returned to his cruiser, Brittany dropped into the passenger seat. She had rage in her eyes like I had never seen before. "Don't you ever, ever tell anyone about my situation," she seethed. "Do you understand?

I don't care what I say or do, don't ever do that again!"

"I'm sorry," I said, realizing I had betrayed her trust. "But he was about to take you to jail."

"That would have been better than being totally humiliated," she argued. "I don't need that stupid cop or anyone else feeling pity for me."

"I'm sorry," I repeated.

The officer drove past us with a curt nod.

Brittany opened the passenger door. "Look, I can drive myself home," she said, starting to get out.

"No, Brittany," I said.

She glared at me. "Do you want to walk, or do you want me to drive you home?"

Knowing the condition she was in, I was tempted to say I'd walk. But I wanted to rebuild the trust between us, so I let her drive me home.

When we reached my driveway, I asked her to stay awhile, but she refused. As soon as I closed the passenger door she sped away, squealing her tires in a huff.

The sky was turning dark. I hoped my friend would make it home safely.

As I walked inside my house, I thought once more about the turn Brittany's life had taken. She was the cutest, most popular girl in school, admired by everyone, and now she had something no one wanted. Sex before marriage was definitely not worth the risk!

I hardly ever let homework consume me, but that night, with so much on my mind, I focused completely on my assignments in an attempt to rid my head of all the issues going on in my world. I was studying really hard when I had an unexpected interruption.

Lance walked into my room carrying three big plastic bags. He set them on my bed and started unloading the contents. One bag had a Dooney and Bourke pocketbook. The second was full of Christian products, including the latest book in the Sierra Jensen series by Robin Jones Gunn, my favorite Christian author. The last bag held clothes from Clothestime. There must have been over two hundred dollars worth of stuff.

"This is all for me?" I asked.

"Yeah," Lance said. "I haven't thanked you yet for what you did for me."

I looked at all the things lying on my bed. "How did you pay for all this?" I asked.

"I had a little money saved up," he said.

"I don't understand." This was definitely out of character for Lance. Every dime he had, he spent on himself. Something wasn't right. "Why did you do this?"

"You didn't rat on me." He shrugged. "I owe you."

"I want you to take it all back," I said, although I was really tempted to at least keep the book.

"What?" Lance cried. "You've got to be kidding."

"I'm not joking, Lance," I said, tearing my eyes from the stash to look him in the face.

"I'm not taking any of it back," he declared. "This is all yours. It's a gift." Before I could say another word, he left my room and closed the door.

The novel drew me. It had been weeks since I finished the last one in the series, and I'd been dying to read the new one. Ignoring the other items, I picked up the book, sat back down at my desk, and started to read, hoping the story would take me away from my problems.

Before I finished chapter one, my parents came in. "So," Dad asked tenderly, "do you want to talk about this thing with Brittany?"

I hesitated. "Um, no," I answered. "Not really."

Mom sat on the edge of my bed. "Sweetie, we know this has to be hard on you," she said with compassion. She reached over and took my hand. "Honey, you're shaking." Her eyes showed so much concern for me, I couldn't hold in my emotions any longer.

"My best friend has HIV disease," I sobbed. "I wish I could take it away, Mom. I wish it wasn't true. What can I do?"

"You've got to pray for her," my dad said in a soft tone. "I'll bet Brittany's thankful you were there for her today."

I wasn't so sure. "I don't know, Dad. She reacted so crazy. She was like a totally different person."

My parents stayed in my room and we talked for a half hour. I was surprised that the dialogue was so real and genuine. My parents were really understanding. They helped me see that my part in this whole thing was to encourage Brittany through the tough stuff she had to deal with.

"That's what friends are for," Mom said. "You need to show Brittany God. She needs to know that Christ is real, and that He wants to save her and change her life."

I looked at my mom and dad through my tears. "I wish Brittany's parents were as understanding as you guys are. She sure needs them right now."

"I'm having breakfast with Brittany's mom tomorrow," my mother said. "Don't worry, Laurel. God wants us to trust Him. And keep praying."

"Your mom's right," Dad agreed. "But He also wants you to realize that some things just aren't worth playing with. Like sex."

"I know, Dad," I assured him. "Believe me, I know."

My father kissed me on my forehead. "Laurel," he said as he started to leave my room, "your life is not a game. It's precious. I know you're smart and I know you make good choices. I'm telling you this because I want you to continue to do so."

I nodded as one more tear dropped.

Brittany didn't go to school the next day, so my mom drove me. I kept quiet all day. When my friends asked what was wrong with me, I couldn't respond.

When I got home that night, I went straight to my room and called Brittany what seemed like a million times, but I kept getting her answering machine. I left a message, but she didn't call me back.

I tried to concentrate on my homework between tries. Suddenly, a loud scream broke the silence in the house.

"No! No! Oh, my gosh!" It sounded like my brother Lance.

I raced to my brothers' bedroom and saw Lance pacing the floor like a crazy person. He was practically pulling his hair out. And he was wearing a brand-new leather bomber jacket that I'd never seen on him before.

"Lance, what's wrong?" I asked.

He turned and looked at me with wild eyes. "I'm in so much trouble. Do you still have that stuff I bought you?"

"Of course. What's going on?"

I heard a cell phone ring. None of us owned a cell phone. But Lance pulled one out of the pocket of his new jacket.

As he answered the call, I looked around his room. I saw quite a few new things, all of them expensive. Where had all this stuff come from? Lance didn't have a job.

"I know," I heard him say into the phone. "I just need an extension. I'll get you the money." He paused, a worried look on his face. "OK, I understand," he whispered, then hung up the phone.

"Lance, what are you into?" I asked.

He turned to me with pleading eyes. "I need some money fast."

"First tell me what's going on, Lance. Talk to me!"

He collapsed onto his lower bunk. "I'm in hot water, Laurel. Really hot. I need a thousand dollars."

"What?" I screamed. "A thousand dollars! What for?"

He buried his face in his hands, and I barely made out his muffled words. "I've been betting on games."

flipping over results

"betting on games?" I shrieked at my brother. "I don't un-derstand, Lance. Are you gambling? Do you have a bookie down your throat waiting for a payoff or something?"

I wasn't letting my brother answer one question before I threw out another. I was livid, and my mind couldn't comprehend the information it was receiving. The idea of Lance gambling was absurd. My dad was a real penny pincher, but the church was doing great and they paid him well enough. We weren't wealthy, but any time Lance needed or wanted anything, he always got it. Why he felt a need for more was beyond me.

Lance stood and started pacing again. "Get off my back, OK?" he grumbled. "I've got enough problems without you adding to them."

I wasn't about to be dismissed that easily. "You'd better answer my questions, Lance, or you're gonna have even more problems . . . with Mom and Dad."

He glared at me. "Why are you in my business?" he mumbled, pulling off the leather jacket and tossing it onto his bed.

I thumped him on the head. "You don't need any *business*. You're only in tenth grade, for heaven's sake! Why are you betting?"

"Shhh!" he said, covering my mouth.

I tried to scream, but he held me tight.

"I'll let you go if you can be quiet," he said.

I nodded my head, but as soon as he let go, I started yelling again. "I can't believe you—"

He covered my mouth again. I rolled my eyes. When he let go, I resumed my lecture, but at a quieter volume. We stood there arguing for about fifteen minutes. Then Liam came barging in.

"What's the problem in here?" he questioned.

Lance and I had not been on the same side all evening, but when Liam came in acting all high and mighty, the two of us quickly joined forces.

"Why do you have to know everything?" I asked him.

"As loud as you two were talking, I didn't know it was supposed to be a secret," Liam said, one eyebrow raised.

"Well, now you know," Lance said as he tried to shove Liam out the door. "So can we have some privacy, please?"

Liam stuck his foot in the doorway. The angry look Lance gave him frightened me. First I had caught Lance drinking. Then I'd caught him gambling. Now he was giving his own brother a look that could kill. What was going on with him?

It occurred to me that I might be in over my head trying to help him. Although Liam got on my nerves, maybe he was right.

"This is my room too," Liam seethed.

"Well, I'm in here now," Lance responded. "Any time you need privacy, I leave you alone. I'm just asking for a little time with my sister. Is that too much to ask?"

When Liam refused to move, Lance grabbed his leather jacket, tossed it over his shoulder, and shoved past his older brother. Liam watched him leave, then turned to glare at me.

"Don't even start," I warned Liam. I tried to leave the room, but he remained in the doorway, blocking my exit.

"Whenever I see you two lately," he said, "you're always in a heated discussion. You can't expect me not to ask what's going on. I don't understand why you guys are trying to keep me out of this."

"Maybe you and I are too close in age to be close as siblings."

He gave me a confused look. "That makes no sense, Laurel."

"See? That's what I'm talking about. You're always trying to analyze everything instead of accepting things at face value. That's why no one wants to tell you anything. You're too judgmental. If no one walks your perfect path, then they're going straight to hell."

Liam's eyes grew wide and round. "That's not fair, Laurel."

I softened my voice a bit. "Maybe it is kind of harsh, but that's how I feel. And I'm pretty sure that's how Lance feels too. You act so perfect, you make us all look bad." In a flash, I realized this was exactly what my Rockdale teammate had accused me of. Ignoring the irony, I continued chastising my brother. "Even the Apostle Paul wasn't as self-righteous as you."

Liam plopped onto his single bed, apparently confident that I was too involved in our discussion to leave. "So you want to have a biblical debate with me now?" he challenged.

I knew I didn't want to go there, so I just mumbled, "Whatever."

Liam stood. "You always say I'm judgmental, but you never really try me. What were you and Lance talking about? Please tell me. I promise I won't flip out."

"I don't know," I said hesitantly.

"You keep covering for him, and you're not helping him. This isn't like you, Laurel. Some shady things are going on with Lance. If he goes down, are you willing to go down with him?"

"You're overreacting," I said, even though I realized he was probably right.

Liam sat back down and patted the bed beside him, inviting me to join him. I sat beside my brother, but on the side nearest the door so I could bolt if he got on my case again.

Liam clasped his hands in his lap and stared at them. "Ever since Lance got on the football team, he's been acting weird," he said softly. "Personally, I think the boy is on drugs."

Liam didn't know how close to the truth he was.

His quiet, concerned words gave me a lot to think about. I knew I couldn't continue carrying this heavy load alone. "Look," I said, "let me pray about this, OK? I want to do the right thing here, Liam, really."

"I know you do," he said.

I got up and went to my room, with no resistance from Liam. I knelt down and gave it all to the Lord. Then I got in bed, laid my head against the pillow, and drifted off to a peaceful sleep.

"Sis, get up!" Lance hollered early the next morning.

I rolled over and looked at my alarm clock. It was an hour earlier than I was supposed to be up. I glared at my brother and grumbled, "Go away."

"But I wanted to tell you that things are OK," he said with a smile. "I'd forgotten about the basketball games. I bet on seven and won five. That gives me enough money to pay off the hockey game. I didn't make a profit, but that's all right. There are plenty of other opportunities coming up."

"You woke me up for that?" I grumbled, rolling over and turning my back to him.

"I just want to thank you for not ratting me out," he continued. "You're the best sister. I won't forget this. Expect another goody bag soon."

I heard him pad out of my room. But I couldn't go back to sleep. I was too furious with Lance. I couldn't believe he was still gambling when he'd just gotten himself out of hot water. He was not learning his lesson, and something had to be done. He needed serious help. I couldn't keep covering for him. I knew gambling could only lead to his destruction.

Friday was the first day of February. Things weren't worse, but they weren't better either. My mom dropped me off at school again, since I still didn't know if Brittany was coming or not. She hadn't been there all week.

When I walked down the hall toward my locker, I saw my friend. I reached out to hug her, and she hugged me back, but just barely. Her body was as rigid as a block of ice. Her face looked as if life had already been sucked out of her. There was no hope in her eyes, no joy in her stance, and no smile on her face.

The bell rang, and I still hadn't gotten the books out of my locker for my first class. I mumbled something about hoping she had a good day, then hurried on to class.

When I saw Brittany at lunch, I was determined not to let it be a somber encounter. We were going to enjoy our break. We were going to enjoy each other. I went over to her enthusiastically and tried directing her to our usual seats.

"Don't touch me," she said coldly.

Her response numbed my heart. "What are you talking about?" I asked.

I couldn't understand what was wrong with her. I had given her some space for a while, but I couldn't let her sulk forever. She didn't have to be so cold toward me.

I noticed Meagan standing behind Brittany, shaking her head. That made me even more curious.

"Brittany," I said without touching her, "come on, let's eat."

She glared at me, her eyes red. "Laurel, if you keep standing in my face, I will probably smack you. Our friendship is over, OK? Do I need to humiliate you like you've humiliated me just so you get the point?"

I stood and stared at her as she searched the cafeteria for a place to sit. I had no idea what she was talking about. But as I looked around, I saw people staring at us in a weird way. *What does everyone know that I don't?* I wondered. Just because Brittany had snapped at me, that was no reason for everyone to gawk at us. Something must have happened. What did I miss?

I decided to play it off, act like I hadn't heard her say that she didn't want to talk to me anymore. "This lunchroom sure is nosy," I said.

"I'm quitting school," she announced without looking at me.

"Why?" I asked.

Her eyes began to water. "Everyone knows."

"Don't be silly," I said. "How could they know?"

She looked at me like a wild animal. "Stop acting like you're not responsible, Laurel!"

Brittany turned away from me, grabbed her stuff from Meagan's arms, and dashed away. I stood there with a blank stare on my face.

Meagan gave me a sympathetic look. "I heard about Brittany," she whispered. "I know her test results."

"You didn't hear it from me," I said.

"I know," she said, looking a little disappointed. "And I understand why you didn't tell me, even though we're friends and we're supposed to share everything with each other."

"Did she tell you?" I asked.

"No," Meagan said. "It's all around school. She's been denying it, but no one believes her. She's devastated." Meagan glanced around the room to make sure no one heard us talking. Then she continued in an accusatory tone. "She said you were the only one who knew about it. You had to have told someone. Honestly, Laurel, I can't believe you would do such a thing to Brittany. You've ruined her senior year." Meagan marched out of the lunchroom in a huff.

I wanted to follow her, to let her know I wasn't a traitor and she must have heard wrong. But I decided to hold off. There's no point trying to talk to someone when they're in the heat of anger. I'd catch up to her later.

I sat down alone at an unoccupied table and opened my sack lunch. As I ate, I overheard people all over the room talking about Brittany and AIDS. I soon got tired of all the gossip and took my lunch outside.

As I was finishing the last bite of my sandwich, one of my classmates, Gretchen Parks, walked up to me. "So," she said, "how does it feel to get even?"

"What?" I asked, peering up at her from my seat in the grass. "I don't know what you mean."

She rolled her eyes at me, as if it was obvious. "Your boyfriend and your best friend were messing around behind your back, and now they both have AIDS."

I held my hand over my eyes so I wouldn't have to squint into the sun. "What do you mean, Branson has AIDS?"

"That's what's going around," she said. "Kind of fitting, huh? Sweet justice and all that. No wonder you told the whole school about it."

I stood so I wouldn't have to talk to her with the sun in my eyes. "Look, Gretchen, I didn't spread anything. And I'm not happy about this."

"You're not?"

"Of course not." I took a deep breath. "First of all, Christians don't hold grudges. Sure, I was hurt when they got together. But I've made peace with that. We're all friends again, and I have a new boyfriend now."

"Yeah, OK," she said, walking away. Obviously, she didn't believe me.

I could understand her disbelief. Foster and I had very busy schedules and hadn't spent much time hanging out together around school. A lot had been going on since Christmas break: the dramas with Brittany and Lance, trying to get back into studying after two weeks off, and doing my best on two different gymnastics teams. So I hadn't been able to spend as much time with my boyfriend as I wanted to. As I made my way to class, I determined to make sure the whole world knew that Foster and I were happy with each other.

When the last bell rang at the end of the school day, I searched frantically for my boyfriend. I wanted to let him know that he was important to me. I also wanted to apologize to him for not being as available to him as a girlfriend should be.

I'd have to hurry. I only had a few minutes before Foster would have to start getting ready for baseball practice in the boys' locker room on the opposite side of the gym. It went against my better judgment to approach him there, but it would only take a minute to tell him what was on my mind.

I crossed the gym floor and found the door to the boys' locker room closed. I didn't know what to do. I walked in circles in front of the door, hoping Foster would come out.

After pacing for a couple of minutes, I heard a somber voice around the corner. "I don't know, Lord," the voice said, obviously unaware that I could hear his prayer. "What if I have it? You've got to fix this for me." I heard a fist smack into the wall. "This is crazy, talking to God," the voice grumbled. "He isn't up there, and even if He is, He sure doesn't hear me."

I knew that voice. "Branson?" I said quietly as I walked around the corner.

I saw him sitting on the floor, his blonde head slumped into his knees. He didn't look up, but I could tell he'd heard me.

"I know this is a private moment," I said. "But I'm here if you need me."

I heard a sorrowful moan, but he didn't move. I wanted to reach out and let him know that God was real and He cared. I walked over and sat beside him.

Finally Branson looked up. His blue eyes shimmered and his face was wet with tears. "I should have listened to you, Laurel," he said, his voice cracking. "I should have been faithful to you, but I just had to have sex. And because of that . . ." He started crying so hard he couldn't finish his statement. He didn't have to.

Branson reached out and wrapped his arms around me. "Please tell me it's going to be OK," he begged.

"It'll be OK," I said, patting his back. "Your first test was fine. You'll see."

He shook his head as it rested on my shoulder. "Laurel, you don't understand. I have to take more tests. I know I'm sick. I can feel it. I'm scared to death."

"You're probably stressing over nothing, Branson," I said, rubbing his trembling shoulder. "Your results should come back negative again."

He pulled back slightly so he could look me in the eye. "When I took the test the first time, I told them about Brittany. They said they would test her, and if I had anything to be worried about, they'd call me." He choked back a sob. "They called me, Laurel," he whispered.

I pulled Branson back into an embrace, trying to give him the comfort he needed so desperately. Even though we were no longer dating, I still cared about him. We'd gone out with each other for two years, and I'd liked him since my first year of high school. I had no desire at all to get back together with him, but I was glad we were still friends.

"I don't know what I'm going to do if the test comes back positive." His voice sounded muffled as he buried his head in my shoulder.

"You're gonna do just what Brittany's gonna do," I said.

"You're going to get some information, and everything will be OK. You can beat this, Branson."

"Yeah, right," he said. "There's no hope for AIDS. The girl I had sex with is HIV positive, and I just know I am too."

Hearing him talk about having sex with Brittany made me feel like I was being betrayed all over again. But I reminded myself that it was over between Branson and me. I had a new boyfriend now, one I could trust never to betray me.

As I sat there, tenderly holding my sobbing ex-boyfriend, I saw Foster come out of the locker room. When he saw me in Branson's arms, his face filled with dejection and despair. Before I could explain, he vanished.

"Branson," I said, gently pushing his head off my shoulder. I really needed to talk to Foster. But when I looked at Branson's devastated face, I knew I needed to stay and try to help him through this. "Can I pray with you right now?" I asked.

He nodded, then bowed his head.

God uses problems to draw us closer to Him. I could clearly see this happening with Branson. He was truly sincere. I just hoped he would continue to seek the Lord.

After a heartfelt prayer, Branson left our meeting encouraged. And so did I.

"But that's not fair!" I exclaimed to Mrs. Turner, my high school gymnastics coach, at the next practice. "You can't pull me from the meet!"

"Laurel, I have to," she said sternly. "What kind of message am I giving if I let you participate in the meet when you've been late to practice twice this week? Even when you are here, your mind is elsewhere. You act like we should all be grateful you show up at all. Laurel, that kind of attitude and performance is simply not going to cut it for this team."

Yeah, right, I thought. *This team has no talent but me. These girls all wish they could perform as good as I do.* I started to walk away.

"Where are you going?" Mrs. Turner asked.

I stopped and turned around. "If I'm not going to compete, I might as well go home," I said angrily. "There's no need for me to practice. It would be a waste of time."

"If you walk out that door, Laurel," my coach warned, "you will not participate in any meets at Salem High School. Do you understand me? Now, you go back out there and practice."

I couldn't believe Mrs. Turner was doing this to me. I was furious, but I didn't want to quit. I had longed for a school gymnastics team ever since I started working with Coach Milligent at the Rockdale County Gym. And I'd been honored beyond belief when Coach Turner asked me to be the new team's captain. No, this was too important for me to let my temper ruin it all. I grit my teeth and took out my frustration on the bars, the balance beam, and the trampoline.

After spending all my pent-up energy, I felt a lot better. I was still disappointed at being cut from the meet, but I'd stopped being angry about it.

"Hey, don't be so down," my friend Shaney said as we changed clothes in the locker room.

"Thanks," I said.

She immediately changed the subject. "So, you remember that guy I liked? Well, I think we're making some progress. Yesterday, in the hall, I dropped my books and he helped me pick them up. Then we started talking, and it was like his beautiful brown eyes mesmerized me. He is so gorgeous."

It was great to hear somebody talk about good news for a change. "That's so exciting," I said. "That's exactly how I met my boyfriend, so I know what you mean."

Her smile dimmed a little. "The bad part is, he told me he had a girlfriend. But I think he's mad at her about something."

"Well, I don't think you should try to break them up," I advised. "But if he's not happy with his girlfriend, then you should be there for him as a friend and maybe he'll take more interest in you. You never know what might happen in the future."

Shaney pulled a brush through her short blonde hair. "He plays baseball, and I was thinking about going to his practice game today. Do you want to go together?"

"Sure," I said. "My boyfriend is on the baseball team, too, so we can watch our guys together. I just have to ask my mom first. But I'm sure she'll say it's fine." I started for the payphone, then stopped and turned around. "Thanks for talking to me, Shaney. I was really bummed about not being able to be in the meet."

"Don't worry," she said with a smile. "After we lose the meet because you're not there, Coach will put you back in."

I really liked this girl. Even though she was just a sophomore, she said all the right things. It was kind of like having a little sister.

"OK, so where is this guy you like?" I said to Shaney when we'd picked our seats at the practice game on Friday after school.

"I don't see him," she said, her eyes searching the field. "Which one is your boyfriend?"

"I don't see him, either."

"That's really weird."

We watched two full innings but still didn't see either of our guys. The practice game was pretty boring without someone special to cheer for. "I'm gonna go get something to drink," I said as the teams switched for the next inning. "You want anything?"

"No, thanks," Shaney said, totally preoccupied with searching for the guy she liked.

When I came back with a cold can of Sprite, Shaney was

bouncing in her seat. "There he is," she squealed, grabbing my arm and pointing to the dugout. "Number seventeen."

I almost choked on my Sprite.

Foster was number seventeen! Her guy was my guy! I thought about our conversation. Thank goodness I'd advised her not to break up that relationship. Still, she had said her guy was mad at his girlfriend, and I'd made her think she had a chance.

I didn't know what to say. I wanted to tell her to forget number seventeen. But she was sitting there bubbling over with excitement like a love-starved puppy, yacking away at how adorable he was. I hated the thought of breaking her heart. So I just kept my mouth shut.

"I want you to meet him," she said after the game was over.

"OK," I said reluctantly.

We stood outside the boys' locker room for a few minutes. I knew I should say something to her, but still couldn't come up with the right words.

Finally, Foster came out. He looked at me for a quick moment, then settled his focus on Shaney. As he walked up to us, she was all smiles.

"So," he said to her, "I see you know Laurel."

"Yeah," she answered, her face glowing. "We're on the school gymnastics team together."

"You do gymnastics too?" he asked her, totally ignoring me.

"Yeah." She giggled. "You should come to our meet. Laurel won't be performing, but you can come see me."

Foster hesitated.

"I mean," Shaney added, "if you think your girlfriend wouldn't mind."

Foster finally looked at me. But there was no warmth in his expression. "What do you think, Laurel? Do you think she'd mind?"

When I didn't answer right away, he turned back to

Shaney. "No, I'm sure she won't." He leaned in closer to her and lowered his voice, but still spoke loudly enough for me to hear. "You see," he told her, "I caught her in the arms of her old boyfriend today, so she can't get angry at me."

Shaney gasped. "I can't believe that!"

"I'm sure it wasn't what it seemed," I said.

Shaney glared at me. I thought for a minute she was going to kick my shin. "Why are you defending her?" she questioned.

I couldn't keep up the charade any longer. I knew if I stayed I'd burst into tears or rage, so I just walked away.

On the way across the gym, I remembered that Foster was supposed to drive me home. But I couldn't go back after our little exchange of words. I went straight to a payphone and called home.

"Liam, could you tell Mom to come get me from school?" I asked, trying not to cry.

I didn't hear his answer because Foster's voice came from behind me. "I'll take you home," he said.

I turned and looked at him. Shaney was nowhere around, and Foster had a sad, confused, hurt look on his face.

"Never mind, Liam," I said. I hung up the phone. "Foster, why are we going through this?"

"I'm sorry if I assumed the wrong thing," he said, taking me in his arms.

I breathed a sigh of relief. "Thank you," I whispered into his chest. "Branson needed me. I just wanted to be there for him as a friend."

Foster looked me in the eye. "Laurel, when we were over there, you didn't like me talking to Shaney all that much, did you?"

"No," I confessed.

"I have no feelings for her at all," he assured me. "But imagine if she was my old girlfriend and you saw me with her like I saw you with Branson. You wouldn't like it any more than I did."

He drove me home in silence. Foster was right. It would

totally bother me if I saw him being close with an ex-girlfriend. There was no way I wanted to get back with Branson. I had only wanted to be a friend to him. But I knew that in order to keep my relationship with Foster going strong, I had to pull back from Branson and focus more time and energy on my boyfriend.

When I got home that night I called Coach Turner and apologized sincerely for my actions and my attitude. She surprised me by deciding to let me perform in the meet. I thanked her about a million times. I arrived early the next morning for the meet so I could practice my routines and try to make up a little bit for the missed practices.

I was determined to do my best. As I mounted the balance beam, the gym became really quiet. I landed every flip, jump, turn, and leap. My beam routine was flawless.

When I attempted my dismount, I stuck it perfectly. I lifted my chin and allowed a huge grin to cover my face. I looked up into the bleachers and saw my parents standing very proudly, applauding with the rest of the fans. Then I looked at Foster, who was nodding his head in approval.

I joined my teammates, and we awaited my score with excited anticipation. When I looked at my numbers and saw I had perfect tens, my knees practically gave way underneath me.

I did great on all the other events as well. I closed my eyes and thanked the Lord for His mercy toward me. I realized I had been very prideful at practice and that my skills were a gift from Him.

After the meet, I headed out to see Foster. As my boyfriend was giving me a hug in the hallway, Branson strolled up. "Laurel," he said, "I need to talk to you."

I looked at Foster, pleading with my eyes for him to understand. I didn't want to upset him, but Branson needed me. I couldn't turn my back on a friend.

Foster gave me a small smile, as if to say that he didn't like it, but he understood. After flashing him a look of gratitude, I led Branson down the hall and around the corner, away from the crowds of people exiting the meet.

"Laurel," he said with a huge grin, "the second HIV test was negative!" He grabbed my waist with both hands, picked me up, and twirled me around.

"That's great," I said, pulling back. "Now, can you put me down?"

"Yeah, sure." His tone became a bit more subdued.

"Thanks." I straightened my shirt, which Branson had mussed up with his excited twirl. "I'm really happy for you."

"Me too," he said with a relieved sigh. "Now I can get on with my life."

"That's great."

Branson got a soft look in his eyes and moved toward me as if he was about to kiss me. I backed up a small step and said, "Well, I guess I'll be seeing you later. My boyfriend is waiting."

"OK." He sounded a little disappointed, but he didn't pursue anything. "See you around, Laurel."

"You bet." I smiled.

When I got back to Foster, he gripped my hand and we walked away. Things were working out great, and I was flipping over results.

f i v e

romancing
the stone

1 ord, if I don't praise you, the rocks are going to cry out,"
I said on my knees while having some quiet time in my
bedroom.

My life was looking pretty good. I was doing great on
both gymnastics teams, Foster and I were relating on a special level, and I didn't have too much drama in my life.
However, my friends did have some issues. Brittany and
Meagan were still angry at me, Lance was still acting weird,
and Shaney was perturbed at me when she found out that
Foster and I were together. But putting all that aside, I had a
lot to be thankful for.

The more time I spent in God's Word, the more I found
to be thankful for. The Lord had already done a lot for me
by sending His Son to die on the cross for my sins so that I
could have everlasting life. That alone was enough to make
me love Him beyond comprehension.

It was February, the month of love. Things were budding

between me and Foster, and my relationship with the Lord was in full bloom. However, I didn't want to get too comfortable. It seemed whenever things started to get good, that's when they started going bad.

"Knock, knock, knock," a familiar voice called from my bedroom doorway.

Before I could say come in, or even open my eyes and turn around, I was thrust off my knees and onto the bed. The impact spun me around and left me on my back so I could stare the culprit directly in the eyes. It was Branson, and he was laughing. Before I could respond, he was on top of me. He had my arms pinned down and was staring hungrily at me.

"Branson," I cried out, trying to wriggle myself free, "what are you doing? Get off me!"

When he opened his mouth to speak, the alcohol on his breath made me want to throw up. "I love you," he whispered. Then he tried to kiss me, but I pushed him away.

"Get off me!" I repeated.

"OK, I'll let you up," he said without altering his position. "But you've got to understand something. I can't go on without you. You've made your point, and I know I did wrong, but you don't need to be with this other guy. You need to be with me."

I pushed against him with my hands and knees. "I'm gonna call my brothers if you don't get off me," I threatened him, knowing that my parents weren't home.

"No one is here but Lance," Branson said. "He let me in."

"That's not true," I said. I had served all three of my brothers lunch less than an hour ago. Since he didn't understand *get off me,* I shoved with all my strength. The force sent him sprawling on the floor.

When I tried to walk out of the room, Branson got up quickly and blocked the doorway. He tried to kiss me again. I pushed him away and smacked him in the face. I smacked him so hard my hand hurt. He stared at me with a blank look.

"Why don't you get it?" I yelled. "Can't you understand that I've moved on? I gave you my heart, Branson, and you broke it!"

"Are you saying you don't feel anything for me?"

I hesitated. I didn't want to lie. "Would it matter if I told you I cared just a little?"

"Yeah," he answered quietly.

"Well, it shouldn't," I said. "Because it doesn't change my opinion of you, Branson. You're drunk, for goodness' sake. Foster is so much more of a man than you are."

I pushed past him and went down the hall to find Lance. I needed to have a serious talk with that boy.

When did Lance start becoming cool with Branson? I wondered. The boys' bedroom was empty, so I started downstairs.

As if my evening wasn't bad enough already, just as I was passing through the living room, the front door opened and in walked Liam, Luke, Meagan, and Foster.

I was glad to see Meagan because we really needed to talk. I wanted to explain about the misunderstanding with Brittany. But I would have to think about that later. First I had to figure out how I was going to explain why Branson was in my bedroom.

"Hey, Laurel," Foster said. "I can't stay long. Just came by to say a quick hello."

"Hi," I said, putting on a smile as I hugged him.

Foster then pulled out a long-stemmed red rose from behind his back. "This is a pre-Valentine's Day gift," he said. "I've got to leave, but I'll call you tonight, OK?"

"Yeah, that'd be great," I said, trying to rush him out the door without appearing pushy.

I took a second to smell the rose, which I shouldn't have done, because in that second, while Foster was waiting for another hug, Lance came up from downstairs, yelling, "Hey, Price! Where are you, man?"

"I'm coming!" Branson hollered back, barreling down

the stairs so fast he almost bumped into Luke. Liam practically had steam coming from his ears when he saw Branson, and he wasn't the only one.

"Hey, you guys joining the party?" Branson asked sarcastically.

"Laurel, what's going on here?" Foster asked, shooting me a tense look.

I was glad he was at least giving me a chance to explain. But before I could say a word, Lance answered the question. "Branson came over here to hang out with me and Laurel," he said innocently.

"Oh, this is gonna be good," Luke teased, settling comfortably on the steps. I told him to go downstairs, and he hesitantly obeyed.

Meagan glared at me, then turned to Liam. "And you wanted me to talk to her?" she said. "She betrayed Brittany with her words, and now she's betraying Foster with her actions."

"Yeah, maybe you shouldn't have brought her over here," I attacked back. "She's just gonna believe what she wants to anyway."

"Well, it's obvious what's going on," Foster said, his voice strained. "Branson was upstairs with you, and the only other person in the house was downstairs." My boyfriend turned to walk out.

I pulled his arm. "No, Foster," I said. "I'm not going to let you walk out on me." His eyes bored into mine, waiting for an explanation. "Yes, Branson and I were upstairs. But I didn't even know he was here. I was on my knees praying and—"

"I don't believe you," Meagan interrupted.

"I was, Meagan." I snapped. "You need to calm down. You're just mad because of that rumor about Brittany you thought I spread."

"What rumor?" Branson asked. "You mean the one about her having AIDS? I'm afraid I started that going. I told my friend Bo, and the next thing I knew the whole school heard about it. Everyone was saying I had it, too, even before I got my results back. I didn't mean to spread Brittany's business. I just told the wrong person."

Meagan looked from Branson to me. "Laurel, I'm so sorry," she said.

I couldn't respond to her at that moment. I still needed to fix things with Foster. "I didn't even know he was coming," I said as I leaned into him.

Foster looked into my eyes and saw that I was telling the truth. Then he turned to Branson. "What's it gonna take for you to realize that she isn't interested in a relationship with you anymore?" he lashed out.

Branson held up his fists to challenge Foster physically. Foster moved quickly around me, raising his fists in acceptance of Branson's challenge. Lance grabbed him, and Liam grabbed Branson. But my brothers' grips weakened as Foster and Branson strained to get to each other. Just as the two angry guys were about to exchange blows, our front door opened and my father walked in.

"What's going on here?" Dad asked, as if what he saw was not explanation enough. "Look, guys," he said to Foster and Branson, "I don't know what's going on or why you're in my house while I'm not here, but this is ridiculous. You are not going to fight in my home. Contrary to what you may believe—" My father looked me in the eye with a disappointed expression. "—young ladies like men with standards, integrity, and honor, not boys playing fist-fighting games."

Dad obviously thought this was all about me, but I knew something else was going on between Foster and Branson. It wasn't just about who gets the girl; it was about who was the bigger man. But I didn't know why Foster had gotten caught up into this.

"Now, I don't know what you guys are going to do to settle this," my father continued, "but I do know one thing. You're going to take this out of my house."

"I'm sorry, Reverend Shadrach," Foster said politely. "I just came to drop off something, but I got held up when I tried to leave. I won't make excuses. I was wrong, and I give you my word it won't happen again." Foster retreated past my father and walked out the door, leaving it open.

"Yeah, I'm sorry too," Branson mumbled, dashing past my father to the door. "Catch you later, Laurel."

Oh great, I thought. *Now my parents will really think Branson came here for me.*

Noticing the tension rising in our home, Meagan said good-bye and took off. She left so quickly that she forgot her purse. I picked it up and was about to try to catch up to her when Lance grabbed it from me and said, "I'll take it to her," thrn rushed out the door.

I knew Lance was just trying to get himself out of trouble by leaving me to face our parents. It was his fault I was in this mess. So I stood there, avoiding my parents' gaze, determined not to get into any discussion until Lance came back. He returned shortly, smiling . . . until he realized he hadn't been gone long enough. We were all still standing in the entryway, waiting for him.

Dad moved us into the living room, which was not a good sign. We only used the living room for serious family discussions. My father took his usual seat in the recliner near the window. I sat on the couch with Lance and Liam on each side of me.

"Dad, I know how this looks," I said before he could speak.

My father fixed me with a sharp look. "Laurel, you don't have to explain anything to me. I can read between the lines."

"Please don't condemn me before you know the whole story," I begged.

Liam cut in. "I don't know what Branson was doing here, but Foster came over with my permission."

"And what right do you have to go against my wishes?" my father scolded his eldest son.

"He was just . . . dropping off a flower."

Dad looked at the rose, which I still clutched in my hand. "Though it seems like a nice gesture," he said in a firm voice, "it's still against the rules. Liam, you're grounded for two weeks."

I thought it was an awfully harsh punishment for a guy who was just doing something nice for his sister. It made me wonder what my consequences would be.

"And what about Branson?" Dad asked, looking directly at me. "Why did you let him in?"

"Dad," I explained, "I was praying in my room, and suddenly there he was. I didn't let him in." I turned to Lance, who was making no attempt to straighten out the situation. "Tell him," I urged him.

Lance shrugged. "Branson was here to see me," he confessed. "I turned around for one second and he disappeared. I didn't mean for anything bad to happen. I totally respect your authority." Lance's reverent tone made my skin crawl because I knew it was fake.

"I appreciate that, Son," Dad said, apparently taken in completely by Lance's act. Then he looked at the three of us for a moment. "Maybe this was all just a misunderstanding."

How pathetic, I thought, fuming at the injustice of it all. *If only he could see Lance's true colors.*

He briefly lectured Lance for not reminding Liam that he shouldn't bring Foster into the house. But basically, Liam was the only one who got into trouble.

Dad finally dismissed us, and Lance headed straight for his room. I followed him, determined to find out what he and Branson were up to. But just as I got to my brothers' bedroom doorway, the phone rang. Since we had Ring Master on the phone line my brothers and I shared, I recognized the distinctive double-ring that meant the call was for me.

"Don't you go anywhere," I said forcefully to Lance. "I have to talk to you."

"Yeah, yeah, yeah," he retorted, lounging carelessly on his bed.

I ran to my room and picked up the phone. "Hello?" I said abruptly.

"Wow," Branson's voice said. "Maybe I should hang up and call back so I can get a warmer response."

"Maybe you should hang up and not call me at all," I said.

"Oh, come on, Laurel," he said. "I know you liked my visit today. It was so romantic."

I hung up the phone with a slam.

Before I could make it back to Lance's room, my phone rang again. I groaned, returned to my room, and picked up the receiver. "Look," I hollered, "don't call me again!"

"I was just calling to say good night," Foster's hurt voice said. "But if I'm bothering you, I'll go."

"I'm sorry," I said, wanting to explain but not knowing how. I was afraid that if I told him I thought it was Branson calling me, he'd get angry again.

"Laurel," he said, "I'm sorry I didn't believe you when you said Branson just stopped by. Seeing him come from your room really upset me. But I shouldn't have challenged him. Anger and pride got to me. Christians don't have to fight to show what they're made of. If anything, fighting just shows how weak you are."

I settled onto my bed and wrapped my arms around my favorite pillow. "It's nice to know you really care."

"I do," he said. "But it seems like every time I turn around, I see you with him. I know it's one-sided. Why doesn't he get the picture?"

I paused, trying to decide if I should explain the latest details. "He was drunk when he came over here today," I finally said.

"What?" Foster cried. "I thought he was acting weird."

"Foster, he was with Lance."

"How does your brother figure into this?"

"You know about Lance getting drunk over Christmas at my grandparents' house, and on New Year's Eve at Brittany's party. Well, he's been gambling too. And ever since Branson hurt his arm in football, he's been acting crazy. Now he's hanging out with my brother. I don't think he's being a positive influence on Lance. They were probably drinking together. I don't know what to do."

"Have you talked to him?"

"Yeah." I sighed. "But it's obviously not working."

"Maybe you should tell your parents."

"I don't want to be a tattletale."

"Laurel," Foster said, "if he does something seriously bad, you'll never forgive yourself."

"Maybe I'm making too much of it," I said.

"Maybe. Or maybe not."

"You're right," I conceded. "I have to talk to him."

Foster hesitated. "Laurel, I don't think I told you this, but I had a problem with drinking in the ninth grade."

"You did?" I was shocked.

"My dad lost his job and was out of work for a long time. He started getting really angry all the time. He even hit me and my mom a few times."

"Oh, Foster!"

"That was before I knew the Lord," Foster explained. "The only thing that seemed to give me any comfort was alcohol. It started with a little sip now and then. But it's hard to stop after just one."

"What made you finally quit?"

"My dad's mom died. From liver failure, caused by her addiction to alcohol. My mom told my dad she didn't want that to happen to him. She threatened to leave him if he didn't stop drinking. He started going to Alcoholics Anonymous, and he found the Lord there. I went with Dad to an AA meeting, and I found God too. I clung to God and He began to change my life."

"Wow," I said, stunned by his story. "For some reason, I guess I just figured you'd been a Christian your whole life."

"Laurel, I don't want your brother to be like I was. You've got to talk to him."

I wanted to ask Foster to talk to Lance, but I didn't know how to ask. Foster took my hesitation as a desire to change the subject. "Did you like the flower?" he asked.

I assured him that I did, very much.

"Then maybe you'd consider going to the Valentine's Day dance with me at the church on Thursday?" he asked sweetly.

"Would I!" Every February fourteenth, our church held a dance in the reception hall. Last year, I didn't go because Branson thought it would be corny. Before we hung up, we prayed. I was so happy that God had given me a boyfriend who had his priorities straight. Our relationship was continuing to be strengthened by the Rock.

"Here," Brittany said, handing me a beautiful pink box. "This is for you."

"What's this for?" I asked. Brittany had been avoiding me for the last couple of weeks and treating me like an outcast. I couldn't help wondering why she was suddenly bringing me a present.

"It's sort of a friendship gift for Valentine's Day," she said. "Just open it."

As usual, she had terrible timing. It was Wednesday afternoon, after school gymnastics practice, and I was standing by the school parking lot waiting for my mom to pick me up. She had promised to take me to the salon to get my hair trimmed for the Valentine's Day dance.

I opened the box. Inside was the most beautiful charm bracelet I had ever seen. Sterling silver with one charm hanging from it—a half heart.

"This is beautiful," I said.

"Read it," she encouraged.

I read the inscription on the heart. "A true friend." I flipped it over and found more engraving on the back. The first line had three letters, L-a-u. Under it was a strange squiggle. Below that were the letters B-r-i-t. "What's this mean?" I asked.

She raised her right hand. On her wrist was a silver bracelet with a half-heart charm just like mine. She placed her half heart up against mine. Together the halves clearly read, "Laurel & Brittany."

"That's great," I squealed. I flipped her charm over, but the other side was blank.

"Where are your words?" I asked. "How come yours doesn't say, 'A true friend,' like mine does?"

Brittany looked embarrassed. "Well," she said, "I'm not a true friend. I haven't treated you the way a true friend should. But I really want to be, Laurel. And I'm really going to try. Someday, when you think I am a true friend, I can go back to the jewelers and get my half engraved."

She was starting to tear up. I became so emotional that I couldn't speak, so I just reached out and hugged her.

"You were there for me," Brittany sobbed, "and all I did was push you away. Meagan told me it was Branson who told my business to the school. I'm sorry for not believing you. I guess somewhere deep down I thought you were happy that I got punished."

"No," I cried. "I was devastated that you got that news."

My mom's van pulled up outside the school. Brittany walked with me to the car. "I'll call you," she said, and we hugged each other.

"I've always been there for you, Britt," I responded with tears in my eyes. "Let's get together soon and go over your options, OK?"

"Yeah," she said with a mixture of sadness and gratitude. "I'd like that."

As Mom drove away, I waved at Brittany, thankful that I

had made peace with her and that she now saw I was a true friend.

––––––––––––––––––––

The night of the Valentine's Day dance, Meagan came over early so we could get ready together. As we put on our makeup, we had a long talk about the misunderstanding with Brittany, and she apologized for not believing me. After hugs of forgiveness, we started trying on our dresses. My mom had bought me a pretty red cotton dress with pink lace. Meagan wore a black-and-white knit outfit that really showed off her figure and her shapely legs.

Meagan stepped out of the bedroom to go to the rest room. I played with some hairstyles but couldn't do much else, because I needed her help with the zipper on my dress. She was gone for almost ten minutes. When I inched my way to the door, I saw Lance in the hallway. He was leaning against the wall with one hand, blocking Meagan from reaching my room. He was speaking too quietly for me to hear his words, but I could tell from his tone he was flirting with his older brother's date!

"Meagan," I called out sharply.

"Laurel," she answered, sounding a little embarrassed. "I'll be right there."

As she shyly ducked under Lance's arm, he turned and whispered in a bad-boy tone, "I'll be at the party with a bunch of guys. I hope I can get a dance with you."

Meagan giggled.

When she got back to my room, I closed the door and confronted her. "What was going on out there?"

"Lance and I were just talking," she said, smiling.

"Liam likes you a lot, you know," I said in a tone that sounded like my parents when they were scolding me. "You shouldn't mislead him if you don't feel the same way."

Her eyes fell. "I know," she mumbled.

"There will be major tension in my house if two of my brothers like the same girl," I added.

She assured me that wouldn't happen.

By the time we reached the church, Foster had told me I looked beautiful about a hundred times. Each time, I thanked him and told him I thought he looked very handsome. And boy, did he! His black slacks, white shirt, and red tie made him look more delicious than a double-fudge sundae with whipped cream and a cherry.

The fellowship hall was decorated beautifully. There were red and pink balloons and construction-paper hearts everywhere. I glanced around the room and figured there were about thirty-five couples there. Fifty tables were set up with white candles surrounded by pink lace, which made everything look romantic. Five of the tables were occupied by chaperones, who were there to make sure we stayed on our best behavior.

As Foster and I wound our way to a free table, I smiled at several of my parents' friends who were seated at the chaperones' table. I was glad Mom and Dad had decided to spend the evening at home alone. I didn't plan on doing anything to be ashamed of or anything, but I did feel more free to be myself around Foster without my parents' supervision.

We were served a three-course meal with our choice of steak and baked potato or Hawaiian chicken over rice pilaf. And we had strawberry cheesecake for dessert. It was all delicious!

As we ate our desserts, a guest speaker, Dr. Charles Stanley, addressed us on the topic of staying pure. His every word spoke to my soul. The message really strengthened my commitment to waiting to enjoy God's gift of sex until after marriage.

After his talk, we were all invited to lift our glasses of sparkling cider in individual toasts. Foster picked up my glass and placed it in my hand, then took his and weaved his arm around mine. "To the girl who has my heart," he said. "Happy Valentine's Day."

"To the guy whose heart belongs to me," I responded.

After we took our sips, he pulled a small gift out of his pants pocket. It was wrapped in shiny pink paper.

It suddenly dawned on me that I hadn't bought anything for him. I felt terrible.

"Open it," Foster urged.

With trembling fingers, I carefully peeled off the wrapping paper. Inside was a tiny square jewelry box. When I opened it I found a beautiful ruby ring. Before I could do anything besides gasp, Foster picked up my right hand and placed the ring on my ring finger.

My heart was so full I couldn't say anything. I just threw my arms around him and gave him a huge hug. Foster always knew exactly what to do to make my heart skip.

As we enjoyed our next dance, I gazed constantly at the ring on my finger. I was romancing the stone.

doing
even better

have you guys seen Meagan?" Liam asked Foster and me as we sat at our romantic table in the beautifully decorated church.

Foster shook his head.

"No, I haven't," I said. "Maybe she went to the ladies' room."

Before Liam walked away, he said with a grin, "Well, if you see her, tell her I went to the car for her present. I'll be right back."

"OK," I told him.

I had never seen my oldest brother look so happy. Meagan was Liam's first real girlfriend, and I was glad he liked someone I knew.

After I watched my brother stroll away, Foster caressed my chin, pulled my face toward his, and asked, "So, how's your night been?"

I smiled with my whole heart. "It's been wonderful. Absolutely perfect." I looked around the room. "Everything's so pretty."

"You're so pretty," Foster said, making me blush. "I don't ever want to disappoint you," he said as he took my hand. "I just want our relationship to get even better and stronger and richer."

"Richer?" I questioned.

"Yeah. The value I place on our relationship is immeasurable. And I want the value to keep growing."

I knew he felt strongly for me. But part of me still compared him with Branson. In most ways, Foster came out way ahead. But I couldn't help asking myself one question. Did I care the same amount for him as he cared for me? I wasn't sure. If I did, wouldn't I have thought to buy him something for Valentine's Day?

I slowly pulled my hand from his grasp.

"What's wrong?" he questioned, in tune with my feelings like always.

I couldn't respond. I was into him, but for a split second I felt crowded. I didn't know what that feeling was all about. But I couldn't lead him on. "I . . . I'll be right back," I said, stumbling over my words and my feet. I needed to get some fresh air. I had to bring reality back into my life.

As I approached the outer door, I saw Liam coming in. "Where are you going in such a hurry?" he asked.

"I just need to get away for a second," I said, pushing past him.

"Have you seen Meagan?" he asked from behind me.

I stopped and turned. "You still haven't found her?"

"No," he said, a concerned look wrinkling his forehead. "I'm getting a little worried."

For the moment, at least, I ignored my own concerns and considered his. "Would you like me to look for her in the ladies' room?"

"Would you?" he responded eagerly.

"Sure," I said, changing my course. He followed me toward the bathrooms. "Don't worry, Liam. I'm sure she's around here somewhere."

I checked every stall in the rest room. When I didn't find her, I became even more determined to find out where she'd gone off to. I didn't want to keep my boyfriend waiting, but I had to keep looking for Meagan. I knew I could explain to Foster later what had happened, and he'd understand.

Liam and I searched every inch of the church, but neither of us found her. I started to really get worried but didn't let on to my brother, because he was worried enough already. We split up to continue the search.

I finally decided to check the parking lot. I didn't see anyone in front of the church, but I heard a very familiar laugh from the side lot. As I ventured over that way, the voices became more distinct. I held my breath to listen more carefully.

When I turned the corner of the church building, I saw Meagan in the arms of my brother. But not my brother Liam. She was with Lance.

I wasn't sure what to do. I didn't want to jump to conclusions and overreact. But I wasn't stupid. There was no reason Meagan should be out here in a dark parking lot hugging Lance. Liam was her date, and he'd been looking all over for her. He had a present for her and everything, and here she was, all wrapped up in Lance's arms as if she were his gift.

Watching the two of them interact stunned me. I felt as if I had tape over my mouth and couldn't say anything. Lance had Meagan pinned against a shiny red convertible and was playing with her hair as if he were some kind of Romeo. She was smiling at him and he was smiling back. When he pulled her head toward his and aimed his lips directly at hers, I knew something horrible was going on.

Before I could say anything, I heard Liam's voice cry out, "What are you two doing?" I twirled around and saw Liam right behind me. Before I could say a word, he tore into me.

91

"And you were out here with them? I thought you were helping me look for my date. You knew she was out here with Lance the whole time, didn't you?"

"No, Liam," I tried to explain. "I just got here."

"I watched you standing there, and you didn't say anything! Don't act like you didn't know."

Meagan and Lance started walking toward us, and I noticed they were both staggering. A beer bottle dropped behind Lance's back.

"You got my date drunk?" Liam shrieked at Lance.

Lance grinned crookedly. "I just took her for a little ride."

Liam's face grew pale. "You've been driving drunk?" he yelled. "You jerk! You don't even have your driver's license yet!"

Lance stood in front of Liam, weaving a bit. "Well, the guy who gave me the keys to his car didn't seem to mind."

Quick as a flash, Liam threw a punch that landed squarely on Lance's jaw. It was so severe it knocked him on the ground. But Lance bounced back up and punched Liam in the gut.

I looked at Meagan. This was all her fault. My eyes heated with anger. Hers were red from drunkenness. I wasn't her mother, so I couldn't scold her for her actions. But I really wanted to tell her how much I hated her tearing my family apart. No true friend would do that.

She touched my arm and started to tell me she was sorry, but I yanked out of her grasp. "I don't have time for this," I seethed as I turned away. She grabbed for me again. I pulled back so hard the force flung her to the ground. From the corner of my eye, I saw her hit the pavement. But at the moment, I didn't care.

I tried to get between my brothers, but a punch landed on my eye. It stung badly, but the shock of what they'd done made Lance and Liam stop fighting.

I stared at my bruised and battered brothers. I could tell

from the way they were looking at me, and from the pain in my head, that my eye was not in good condition. It soon swelled shut.

My brothers both started apologizing to me, and Lance suggested we all go home. As we headed for the car, Meagan called from behind us, "Hey! How am I supposed to get home?"

"Find your own ride," Liam tossed over his shoulder as the three of us hopped into Dad's Cadillac Seville.

As we pulled out of the parking lot, I suddenly realized that I hadn't said good-bye to Foster. "We've got to turn around," I said suddenly. "Foster's still at the church."

"Don't be silly, Laurel," Liam said. "You can't go back in there looking like that."

"Is my eye that bad?" I questioned.

"Yes, it's that bad," Lance responded. "I can't believe he hit you."

"I didn't hit her," Liam protested. "You did!" The two of them started arguing again. Liam swung at Lance in the backseat, and the car swerved on the road.

"Stop it," I screamed. "Let's just get home!"

I couldn't wait to get back to my own bedroom. But I was a little apprehensive about facing my father. All he'd asked of us before the dance was that we carry ourselves with respect. Seeing us this way would really tear him apart.

Liam broke the silence in the car. "I'm gonna tell Dad about your drinking problem. But he doesn't have to know I hit you."

"Why not?" Lance taunted. "Because you want to look like the good little Christian who never gets in trouble? Wouldn't suit your image for Dad to know you hit me over some girl?"

Liam's jaw tightened. "I hit you because you were driving drunk. Man, you could have killed her!"

"I could have killed *her*?" Lance hollered. "So you don't care about me killing myself?"

"Hey, if you want to be stupid and take your own life, then no, I don't care."

"You don't mean that," I said. "Lance, he doesn't mean that."

Lance shrank down in his seat. "Yeah, say whatever you want. I know he doesn't care about me. That's why I didn't have a problem making out with his girl."

Before Liam could react, I said, "Guys, we're family. We can't let anything come between us." I lowered my voice and said to Liam, "I agree with you about not telling Dad about the fight. But do you really think we should tell him about Lance's drinking?"

"Don't even start with me, Laurel," Liam said. "You knew he was having these problems before I did, so part of this is your fault for not telling on him in the first place. But I'm not letting him get away with this." He looked at Lance through the rearview mirror. "Brother, you'd better believe you're going down this time."

"So tell," Lance said. "I don't care. It'll be your word against mine. And Laurel isn't going to say anything."

Liam glared at me. Then he shook his head. "You know what? I won't say anything either. Be stupid and ruin your life if you want."

We rode the rest of the way home in silence. When the three of us dragged ourselves through the front door, we found Mom sitting on the couch watching a movie.

"What happened?" she asked as she leaped off the couch toward us. My brothers had turned their faces, but I hadn't thought that quickly. "Look at you, Laurel. Oh, my goodness! Your face looks awful. Dave, honey," she called toward the kitchen.

As my mom did a close-up examination of my eye, Dad came into the room. "What's going on?" He walked up to Lance and Liam and noticed their marks right away. "Answer me, boys."

When they didn't say anything, Dad turned to me.

"Laurel, I want an explanation. I send you three to church for a social, and you come back all beaten and bruised. Explain this to me."

I didn't want to betray my brothers. I couldn't tell my father they had gotten into a fight on church grounds, and I sure didn't want him to know alcohol was involved. But in spite of my resolve, I just started to talk. I guess my heart knew my brothers were in turmoil, and my father needed to straighten this out. I told him about the fight, leaving out any mention of alcohol.

Mother groaned and collapsed back onto the couch.

Dad glared at my brothers. "Is this true?" When they didn't admit it or deny it, he continued. "Let me get this straight. You were fighting over a girl, and your sister tried to stop it, and you hit her?"

"Dad," Liam said, "Laurel isn't as innocent as she sounds." I gasped, but Liam kept talking. "Yes, I threw the first punch. But I was fighting Lance because he'd been driving drunk. I admit, I should not have lost my temper, but what he did made me furious. Your jock of a son is an alcoholic, Dad. And Laurel has known about it since Christmas, but she's been hiding it." He turned to me, his face red. "Admit it, Laurel."

"Dad, don't listen to him," Lance begged.

"Hush, Son," Dad said, then he turned to me. "Laurel, what is Liam talking about?"

I pressed my lips together. I'd said all I was going to say, and Liam couldn't force me to admit any more.

But Liam wasn't finished. "When we were at Grandpa's house, the reason Lance had to go to the emergency room was because he drank too much and cut his hand on a broken glass. He was drunk on New Year's Eve too. And when Branson was over here the other day, Lance was drinking with him."

Dad looked at Lance for a long, silent moment. Then he turned his attention back to Liam. "If you knew all this, why didn't *you* tell us?"

Liam didn't flinch. "Because I wasn't sure until tonight. But Laurel was in on it."

Dad gave me a withering gaze. I looked at my mom, but she turned away from me. I could tell her heart had been broken into pieces by hearing this news about her children. Though I hated Liam for saying what he did, I knew every word was true.

"Laurel," my dad asked, "how would you feel if Lance had killed himself or someone else because of his drinking?"

I couldn't answer. I had never really thought about that. But when my father put it that way, I could clearly see that I had made the wrong choice.

"Laurel, Liam," Dad said, "please go to your rooms. Your mother and I need to talk to Lance alone."

I walked to my room, feeling sick to my stomach. I had let my parents down in a major way. I thought I was doing the right thing by concealing Lance's problem, but I had just made it worse. And we hadn't even mentioned his gambling.

As I sat in my room, I stared at the ruby ring and thought about Foster. How could I have just left him at the dance? What must he be thinking?

I reached for my phone, hoping he'd be home, but it rang before I could pick it up. I answered before the ring stopped. "Hello?"

"So, you're home," Foster said frigidly.

"Yeah," I said, shaking. "I got in a little while ago."

"OK, I was just checking. Good night."

"Wait!" I listened for a click, but didn't hear one. "Can I explain?"

Foster sighed. "I'm kind of tired right now. I'll call you some other time." He hung up. It was a quiet click, so he hadn't slammed down the phone. But I knew he was irritated with me, and I couldn't see how to reconcile it.

What am I going to do? I wondered. How could I explain to my boyfriend why I'd left him alone at the dance?

I knelt beside my bed and prayed silently. *Lord, thank You for Your grace. Thank You for forgiving me for all my mistakes. I don't know why I can never be satisfied with what I have. Paul said in Philippians 4 that he had learned to be content. Teach me this, Lord! And please help me with Foster, Liam, Lance, my dad, and my mom. Show me in Your Word how to handle this mess, and I promise to listen to You from now on.*

I felt safe on my knees talking to the Lord, and I didn't want it to end. But I finally pulled myself up and went to sleep, knowing that God was holding us all in the palm of His hand. He had everything under control, which gave me comfort.

My parents grounded me for two weeks. No going out, no friends allowed over, and no phone privileges. Mom and Dad didn't even try to conceal their disappointment. They didn't treat me badly, but I wasn't their best friend, either. When they asked me about the ring on my finger, and I told them Foster had given it to me for Valentine's Day, they didn't even act excited. Then again, neither did I.

At school I tried to avoid people as much as possible, but everyone wanted to know how I got that black eye. I just told them it was an accident and didn't offer any more information. When they gave up on that subject, they begged for details on my new ring. I said it was a gift and came up with some excuse to walk away.

I particularly avoided Meagan, and Foster made a point of avoiding me. By the end of the week, my black eye faded to a yellowish green, but the left side of my face was still tender. People stopped asking about it, although I caught them staring at me several times.

The following Wednesday, on my way to second period, I stopped Foster in the hallway and refused to let him pass until he said something to me.

Finally giving up, he sighed. "I know I haven't been

talking to you, Laurel, but that's because I didn't want to. Don't you know how embarrassing it was to be left at the dance? I was going crazy wondering what happened to you."

"Foster, I—"

"I couldn't imagine that you'd leave without telling me. And you didn't give me a Valentine's Day gift, either."

The ruby ring felt heavy on my finger. "I'm so sorry, Foster. I—"

"You know what?" he said, cutting me off, "I'm still not up to talking about this. Maybe I should be more forgiving, but I just don't want my girlfriend treating me the way you did. Maybe we should reconsider our places in each other's lives." I was so stunned, I couldn't move. He darted around me and down the hall.

When my focus cleared, I realized that several spectators had been looking on. It felt as if I was in a gymnastics meet and I had taken a huge fall. A true gymnast would get back up and try again. I had to get my life together—with God's help, of course.

I walked quietly to the bathroom to talk to the Lord. I asked Him to reveal His way to me. I asked Him to show me how to please Him and no one else.

———————

On the first Friday night after my restriction was lifted, Brittany invited me to spend the night. "Thanks," I said as we nestled on her bed. "You have no idea how bad it is at my house. It's like a prison. My parents are so mad at me."

"It doesn't make any sense," my friend commiserated. "I can't believe they're blaming you. You're not responsible for telling them your brother's every move."

"I know," I cried, throwing my hands up. "But then, if I didn't tell what I knew, and my brother got hurt, I would've felt horrible." I shook my head at the futility of my situation. I'd thought it over all week and still hadn't come up with a good answer. I shook it off. "Enough about me, how are you doing?"

Brittany lowered her head. "It's still hard for me to talk about my condition. I'm so embarrassed."

"You don't have to be embarrassed around me," I said, taking her hand.

"I know, Laurel," she said with a sad smile. "But it's still really hard. I'm learning a lot about the disease. The doctors are monitoring me, and I'm taking that medication."

"Do you feel different?" I asked carefully. "I mean, physically?"

"Yeah," she said. "During cheerleading, I get tired doing the jumps and stuff. I told my doctor about it and he gave me iron tablets. He told me I'll probably live a long, healthy life if I continue to take care of myself."

"Well, then," I said, squeezing her hand, "you'll just have to take care of yourself, OK?"

We talked and prayed and enjoyed each other's company for several hours before drifting off to sleep.

When I woke up in the morning, Brittany drove me to my gymnastics practice at the Rockdale County Gym. Before I got out of the car, she grabbed my hand. "I don't know what I would have done without you," she said, tears forming in her eyes. "I know you've been praying for me, and I thank you for that. I can't change the fact that I'm HIV positive. But thanks to you, my life is going on."

"That's great," I said, giving her the warmest hug ever.

———————————

When I got home from practice, I saw Liam in his room, reading the Bible. We hadn't talked about anything serious since the night of the dance, so I decided to see if I could clear things up between us.

I sat on his bed and watched him at his desk until he looked up. "So, how are you and Meagan doing?"

"Actually, I'm fine," he answered, a bit too quickly. "I've

come to realize that I was putting the kind of trust in her that I should only put in God. I can't afford to think that some cute girl can do more for me than my Savior."

I nodded. "I think I was making too much out of Foster too," I said, staring at the ruby ring on my finger. "Maybe the reason I got so freaked out that night was because my spirit knew I wasn't ready for what he was offering."

Though it was tough for both of us to admit, God had gotten out of place in our lives. I hoped that would never happen again. I also hoped that Liam and Lance could work out their differences.

I hugged my brother and went into the den, where my parents were talking. I knew I needed to confess some things to them. When they saw me in the doorway, they stopped chatting and gave me their full attention.

"So," I started, "I just want you guys to know that I've thought about it, and I realize now that I was wrong for not telling you about Lance's problem." Their faces softened as they smiled at me.

"You know, Laurel," Mom said, "what upsets us most is the fact that you and your brothers felt you couldn't talk to us. We love you all, and we've been there for you countless times in the past. We want to guide you and help you with your problems. But we can't do that if you keep shutting us out."

The only thing I could do was hug her. The moment was so real. Not everything was right yet. Foster was still mad at me, Meagan and I weren't talking, and Liam and Lance hadn't patched things up. But Brittany and I were re-building our friendship, and the wall between me and my parents was slowly coming down. Things weren't perfect, but they weren't horrible, either. As I looked at where I'd come from in my Christian walk, I knew I was doing even better.

standing
my ground

as I walked down the hall toward my room, I heard Liam and Lance arguing over who was going to use the bathroom. I peeked through the crack in the door.

"I was brushing my teeth," Liam complained at Lance. "You can't just barge in here and use the toilet!"

"I can and I did," Lance proclaimed, zipping up his pants. "I've done it before, and you never had a problem with it. Suddenly you get a girlfriend, and you think everything is all private. Hey, maybe that's the problem. You never noticed before that your little brother has grown up. My friends on the football field say I'm packing more than you can understand. That's probably why your girlfriend's been looking at me."

Liam started shaking. I was blown away by Lance's tough talk. He'd never been so straightforward, and I wasn't sure it was a good thing at all.

I pushed the bathroom door open a bit farther. "This is

ridiculous," I said. "You're brothers and you're acting like enemies. You can't let anything come between you guys, especially not a girl."

"This isn't about Meagan," Liam retorted. "This is about respect. My little brother here thinks he doesn't have to give me any."

"So what are you gonna do?" Lance asked. "Beat it out of me? Are you going to hit me again, or let Big Sister do it for you?"

"You shouldn't be involved in this, Laurel," Lance told me.

"Yeah," Liam agreed. "This is between us. Why don't you just get out of here?" Liam pushed me out of the room and closed the door.

Though the bathroom wasn't very large, I wanted to be in the midst of all the drama. I wanted to explain to them that their behavior was unacceptable. They had to find their way back to each other, and if they couldn't do it on their own, I would have to help them.

I opened the door and boldly stepped back in. "OK, so this isn't totally about Meagan," I said. "But whatever this is about, you guys are brothers—"

"Yeah, brothers who have never gotten along," Liam quipped.

"And now that I'm coming up," Lance said to Liam, totally ignoring me, "you're getting jealous. You can't push me down anymore and tell me to wait for my turn."

"Hey," I said, holding up my hands in surrender, "if you guys want to be stupid, go for it. Just let me get out of your way so I won't get hit again."

"No, Laurel," Liam said, throwing his toothbrush into the sink. "You don't have to leave, because I'm leaving. I've had about as much of this as I can take."

"Fine, leave," Lance shouted as Liam headed for the door. "Better move, Laurel."

When I wouldn't budge, Liam shouted, "Get out of my way!"

I was sick and tired of the way they were treating each other, but I was more upset with the way they were treating me. I was not a doormat or a punching bag. I didn't have to put up with this!

Suddenly, I totally lost control and told both of them off. I railed on them until I was red in the face, and their cheeks turned pale as they listened to me.

"Well?" I finally said, my hands on my hips. "What have you two got to say, huh?"

They didn't apologize to each other, but they did tell me they were sorry for the way they'd treated me. I figured that was good enough for a start.

I stomped to my room, my heart heavy. Even though my brothers had calmed down, I had blown it. James chapter one says that the anger of man does not achieve the righteousness of God. Losing my self-control was not the right way to handle the situation. However, I thanked God that, in spite of me, He had used my anger to defuse my brothers.

The more I thought about it, the more I realized that I wasn't just mad at them. I was tired of the way a lot of people were treating me.

My parents acted as if I was to blame for Lance's problem. Maybe I should have told them, but it wasn't my responsibility to keep tabs on my brothers.

Foster was acting like a big baby instead of understanding about my family problems. Sure, I should have told him I was leaving the church, but he should have known when he saw me with a black eye that something strange had happened. He didn't even ask me about it.

Meagan had been calling constantly. I knew she wanted my forgiveness, but I just couldn't give it to her yet. She had ruined my family. Well, she'd caused a lot of drama, anyway.

Though I was beginning to stand stronger, I knew I

couldn't fix the world's problems. I could only try to fix mine and leave the rest to God.

Branson grabbed me in the middle of the hallway at school. "I have to take one more test," he said.

"OK," I replied. "But what does that have to do with me?" The bell had already rung, and I knew I was going to be late for class.

"This is a big one, Laurel," he said, his eyes wide. "If I've got . . . you know . . . it'll show up on this one. I really need you to be there for me."

I sighed. "Branson, I didn't help you get into this situation, and it's not my job to hold your hand while you try to get out of it." I started to walk away, but he grabbed my arm.

"I know," he said quietly. He looked around to make sure no one was standing close enough to hear us. "Don't you understand how hard it is for me to come to you for support? I know now that if I would have been honorable in our relationship, I wouldn't even be in this situation."

The sincerity in his voice moved me. I thought about how Christ would handle this. I wanted to be there for Branson as I had been before, but we both needed to move on from that. He had to grow up and learn how to face reality without me. Perhaps God was using this severe test to draw Branson to Himself. Sometimes, when people hit rock bottom, that's when they finally realize their need for God.

"What do you want me to do?" I asked with a sigh.

He reached out and twisted a strand of my hair between his fingers. "I'm not asking you to go with me." He gave me a small smile. "In fact, I think you might even be bad luck."

"What do you mean by that?" I asked, pulling my hair out of his grasp.

"Well," he said, "when you went with Brittany, she got less than favorable results."

"Branson, you cannot believe that my presence had anything to do with the outcome of her test. If you really believe in luck, you don't understand anything about who God is. He is in control of all things, and that eliminates luck."

"Take it easy," Branson said, his smile growing a little. "I was just kidding."

I shook my head and took a deep, exasperated breath. "So, what do you want me to do for you this time?"

He paused, his smile disappearing. "I just want you to pray with me."

"What?"

"I want you to pray with me," he repeated. "Will you?"

I had been praying for Branson a lot but had never prayed with him. What was going on with him? Was he for real? He had never wanted us to pray together before, even when we were going out.

"Are you OK?" he asked.

"Yeah," I said. "I'm just blown away."

His smile returned. "But in a good way, right?"

"Yeah," I told him with a chuckle. "Definitely."

He reached out to hug me. I returned his embrace, expecting it to be a simple expression of friendship. But soon I felt his hands rubbing up and down my back. A voice inside me yelled, *Stop this right now!* But the voice was small and quiet, and I chose to ignore it.

"You're going to be fine," I whispered in Branson's ear. I didn't know why I was saying that when I wasn't sure. But I wanted to make him happy. For some strange reason, I was experiencing feelings for him that I'd thought were long gone.

As I stood there, enjoying Branson's embrace, I heard Foster's voice behind me. "Why are you hugging him?"

Branson and I released each other quickly as my brain searched for an explanation. Unable to come up with anything, I huffed, "So, now you're finally talking to me?" Trying to shift the blame from myself to him, I added, "It took me being with my ex for you to notice me?"

"Dang!" Branson commented. "You obviously don't know how to communicate with your girl, man. Why don't you take some lessons from me? We were understanding each other very well until you came over here."

I glared at my ex-boyfriend. "That's enough, Branson. We'll talk later."

"But . . ."

"But what?" I asked, frustrated.

"We didn't pray."

I closed my eyes for a moment. "Branson, please—"

"OK, I'll call you," he said. He gave me a quick kiss on the cheek and hurried away. I turned to face Foster.

"Laurel, what's going on?" he asked quietly. "You're supposed to be in class, and you're out here talking to your ex-boyfriend."

"Aren't you supposed to be in class too?" I asked, still trying to skirt the real issue.

"I had to go to the bathroom," he said, waving a hall pass.

"Just because you saw me hugging him," I argued, "does that give you a reason not to trust me? Maybe if you'd talk to me once in a while, you'd know what's going on with my life. But you've been so distant. Heck, you've been absent!"

"Don't jump down my throat," Foster said. "Maybe I was wrong."

I raised an eyebrow. "Maybe?"

"OK, I was wrong. But being left at a dance is pretty embarrassing."

"Since when do you care about what other people think?"

"Don't turn this around, Laurel. Are you going to tell me what's going on with you and Branson or not?"

I rolled my eyes. "Nothing is going on. He just needed to talk. The same as he did before."

Foster shook his head. "How is it that you can be there for a guy who has hurt you, yet you don't ever talk to me?"

"Foster, I've tried to talk to you," I said. "But you keep slamming the door in my face. I don't know where we stand . . . or if we stand at all."

His face flinched. I knew my words had hurt deeply. "Well, from what I saw, it doesn't seem like you care if we have anything left. You seemed quite happy with Branson."

I looked him square in the eye. "Well, you're assuming the wrong things."

"Am I? Be honest, Laurel. You were acting a little weird even before you left the dance. Something has been bothering you for a while now, hasn't it?"

Foster was right. Things were bothering me. I didn't know what was going on between us, but I knew I had to fix it.

"So, where do we go from here?" Foster asked.

I was glad he'd posed the question. It gave me a chance to make some decisions. We weren't married, so I was under no scriptural obligation to follow him. I was supposed to follow God alone. But now that Foster had asked me straight out, I felt confused. I didn't know what to say. "I don't know," I whispered.

"Well, when you've figured out what you want, give me a call, OK? I'll be around."

I watched him walk away. It felt good to know that he was thinking about me. But what was he thinking? Did he believe we should work things out between us, or was he considering just dropping me?

Lord, I prayed as my footsteps echoed down the empty corridor, *work this out the way You want it to be. I can't do anything but stay still and wait for You to guide me. Please help me out, because I feel like I'm going in the wrong direction. Thanks.*

As I neared the physics classroom, I remembered it was lab day. In one way, that was a relief. Maybe the teacher wouldn't notice my absence as he worked with other students on their projects. Unfortunately, my lab partner was Meagan. We hadn't spoken since the night of the dance, and I still wasn't ready to deal with her.

When I peeked inside the classroom, I noticed the instructor had his back to the door, working at one of the student tables. I snuck in quietly.

The first face I saw was Meagan's. When she started walking toward me, I wanted to bolt in the opposite direction.

"Laurel," she whispered, "please give me a chance to explain."

"Fine," I said, getting the supplies I needed for our physics project out of my desk. "What do you want to say?"

"Laurel, I know you're mad at me, and I don't blame you," she said quietly, pretending to be working on the project with me. "I didn't plan this. The way Lance acted toward me just made me want to go to him. I can't explain it. I didn't want to come between Liam and Lance, and I would never want to disappoint you."

I could understand what she was saying, and I knew I needed to forgive her. But I wasn't ready to discuss it. When I saw the teacher looking toward us, it gave me the excuse I needed. "Look, Meagan," I said, keeping my eyes on the desk, "this isn't the time or place to talk about this."

"Well, when, Laurel?" she persisted. "When can we talk?"

"I don't know," I said. I walked up to the teacher and requested a new lab partner. To my disgust, Mr. Schalett refused.

I returned to Meagan and said, "Let's just get this done."

"I understand," she said sadly.

I felt kind of weird being distanced from Meagan, but I couldn't help it. My brothers were fighting every day, and it was her fault. That was enough for me.

Lord, I prayed, *if my heart is too hard, make it softer.*

When the bell rang, Meagan asked if we could go somewhere to talk.

"It's Thursday," I reminded her. "I've got practice at Rockdale." I jetted off for Brittany's car before Meagan could say another word.

"Ouch!" I said as I landed on my behind after falling from my vault.

Miss Weslyn, the assistant coach for the Rockdale team, rushed over and helped me to my feet. "Laurel, what's going on with you?" she asked. "You're coming up with great routines, but you haven't been sticking your landings at all. You have to follow through."

"I need a break," I said, rubbing my backside.

"OK, take five," she said. "Go to the bathroom and come back with a clear head. I know you're a busy girl, but I need you to be all here during practice time."

"Yes, ma'am," I said, then headed to the bathroom.

Life was getting hard. The previous Saturday Coach Milligent had told me that the girls I would have to compete against to make the U.S. Olympic team were far ahead of me. That news had really deflated me. I was at the top of my game, and I still wasn't good enough. There didn't seem much point in competing if I was going to get a 9.5 and the other contenders got tens.

When I opened the door to the bathroom, I headed straight to the sink and splashed cold water on my face. That usually revived me, but instead I felt lightheaded. I grabbed a paper towel to wipe my face, and the dizziness got worse. I shook my head, wondering what was wrong with me. When I looked in the mirror, everything was cloudy.

Then I noticed a tangy, smoky aroma all around me. So I wasn't losing my mind. I wasn't sure what pot smelled like, but I knew it wasn't cigarette smoke. I crouched down and saw feet in one of the end stalls. I softly knocked on the door.

"Go away," a groggy voice said.

I couldn't make out who it was, so I knocked again.

"Someone is using this! Go away!"

When I knocked on the door a third time, it sprang

open. Kirsten Wells stood there, her coppery green eyes glazed.

"You're wrecking my party, girl!" she said.

Kirsten was my biggest competition on the team. She'd always been level headed, but right now she was not acting like herself. She was so stoned that she didn't realize how much trouble she was in.

"What are you doing?" I asked.

"Want some?" Kirsten teased, holding her little treasure out to me. "Good girl wanna turn bad?"

I tried to snatch it from her hand so I could put it out. But she must have guessed my intention. She flew out of the stall and braced herself against the sink.

"Why are you doing this?" I asked.

"Laurel, please don't tell," she begged.

Before she could move again, I grabbed the joint out of her hand. Just then Coach Weslyn walked in. "Laurel," she said, "what's taking you so long?" When she saw the joint in my hand, her face went pale. "Laurel Shadrach, what are you doing? You could get kicked off the team for this, you know."

"I can explain," I whimpered, dropping the smoking stub into the sink.

"Kirsten, get back out there. Coach Milligent is looking for you. I need to talk to Laurel alone."

Kirsten raced out of the room without a backward glance. Then Coach Weslyn lectured me for five minutes straight. When she finally took a breath, I said, "Listen, OK?" She paused. "This isn't mine. I know you probably think I'm ratting out a teammate, but Kirsten was the one who had this."

"Laurel, you were the one holding it when I walked in. Don't blame someone else."

"I would never do that," I said, getting angry. "I've been on this team for years, and you ought to know me well enough to know I don't smoke pot. I just took it from

Kirsten so I could put it out. I thought you and I had a closer relationship than this." I glanced at the smelly, burning cigarette. "I know I've had some problems, but I would never resort to this."

Coach Weslyn started to apologize, but I was in no mood to hear it. I left her in the cold, smoky rest room.

As I walked out, Kirsten cornered me. "You told on me, didn't you? I know you didn't take the rap for me."

"And why should I?" I asked. "That wouldn't solve your problem."

"You said you wouldn't tell on me," she pouted.

"No, you asked me not to tell on you," I said, allowing my disgust to show in my voice. "If you hadn't been high at the time, maybe you'd remember our conversation more clearly."

Two of the other girls on the team gathered around us, trying to hear what we were saying. When I stopped speaking, Amanda asked quietly, "Kirsten, what's wrong?"

"Laurel told on me," Kirsten said. "She's not a team player at all."

"Why didn't you give her some?" Janet whispered.

"Have you guys been smoking too?" I asked, amazed.

Amanda looked at me with narrowed eyes. "Are you gonna tell on all of us now?"

"Why would you do this?" I said. "Don't you know pot affects your health and your mind?"

Janet rolled her eyes. "Look, Goody Two Shoes. We get a lot of pressure from you and Coach Milligent. It makes our lives easier if we can tune you both out once in a while." Kirsten giggled.

"Yeah," Amanda agreed. "And when we're more relaxed, we do better with our routines."

"Marijuana doesn't make things easier," I said. "It only makes you think you're doing better. Besides, being good in gymnastics is not more important than your health."

I wanted to tell them that getting high wasn't really living. That real life, real joy comes from knowing God and obeying His Word. But how could I tell them that when I didn't always follow the Word of God myself? I needed to stay by God's side continuously. To lead a victorious Christian life, I needed to start standing my ground.

slipping into dizziness

S top moving, you guys," Kirsten said as our team stood on the blue mat waiting for Miss Weslyn to return from her talk with Coach Milligent.

"We're not moving," Amanda said.

I could tell by the pasty look on Kirsten's face that something was wrong. She was off balance and sweating heavily. She looked at me with bloodshot eyes. "Laurel, I . . . I don't feel so—"

I caught Kirsten in my arms before she passed out on the ground. Janet and Amanda screamed.

"You guys stay with her," I yelled. "I'll go get help." I passed Kirsten's limp body to the other girls and raced to Coach Milligent's office. "Coach!" I hollered as I barged in.

He rose to his feet. "Laurel, what's wrong?"

I stood there, trying to catch my breath. "Call 911! There's something wrong with Kirsten."

Miss Weslyn made the call while Coach Milligent followed me to Kirsten.

"Does anyone know what's wrong with her?" he asked.

Janet glanced at me, trembling. "It was just a little weed, Coach," she admitted. "I had some, too, but I'm fine."

Amanda's voice from behind me yelled out, "Janet, don't!"

"Who said that?" Coach Milligent demanded. "Carson, is that you?"

"She swore me to secrecy, Coach," Amanda cried.

"Carson, take a good look at this girl. She could lose her life right here! Now, tell me what's going on!"

Tears streaked Amanda's face. "Kirsten's been taking a lot of pills," she said. "I saw her sorting them in the locker room one day. I told her it was wrong, but she promised me it would be OK."

After what seemed like hours, but was probably only minutes, a team of emergency workers came rushing into the gym. They immediately put an oxygen mask over Kirsten's mouth. But instead of stabilizing her, it sent her body into convulsions.

"She's in shock," the paramedic said. "We've got to get her to the hospital." He looked at Coach Milligent. "Have her parents been notified?"

"Yes," Miss Weslyn said. "Her mother is on the way here."

"When she arrives, tell her to meet us at City General," the paramedic said, rushing Kirsten out the door on a stretcher. Coach Milligent and Miss Weslyn followed.

"Please, Lord," I prayed aloud in the silence that followed. "Please help Kirsten."

Janet sauntered over to me. "This is all your fault. You did this to her. I hope you never sleep!"

Before I could say anything to her, Janet ran after the gurney carrying Kirsten. The rest of the girls looked at me with the coldest stares I had ever received in my entire life.

Their eyes cut through my heart sharper than scissors cutting paper. Then they left me in the gym alone.

As I looked around the room, tears clouded my eyes. Was this all my fault? Had I raised the level in gymnastics so much that the girls felt they had to turn to drugs to compete?

As I leaned over the bar, dazed, a pair of warm arms wrapped around me. I turned and saw my mother. Coach Weslyn must have told her what was going on, because she looked at me with sad, loving eyes. She said nothing. Neither did I. I just buried my head on her shoulder.

Finally, I whispered, "This is all my fault."

"No, it's not," Mom said in a soothing voice.

"It sure feels like it is. The girls all blame me. They think I was so good that Coach Milligent made it tough on them."

"Now, honey, you know that's not true." My mother stroked my hair. "Come on, sweetie, let's go home."

I looked up at her. "I can't go home yet. I've got to go to the hospital to make sure Kirsten is OK."

"Why don't we just go home and call the hospital?"

"No," I insisted. "All the other girls will be there, and I know they don't want me around, but I need to go. Please, Mom. Take me to the hospital."

She brushed tears off my cheek. "Laurel, look at yourself. You've made yourself sick over this. You can't stress out like this. You need to go home. I'll make you some tea."

"Mom, please . . ."

She looked into my eyes and read my desperation. "OK, we'll go to the hospital."

After hours of pacing in a crowded waiting room filled with beautiful young gymnasts with devastated faces, the doors from room C opened slowly. Kirsten's parents and the two coaches had entered that room a long time ago, leaving the rest of us to wonder. A woman in a white jacket came out and walked toward us.

"Ladies, I'm Dr. Sinclair," she said. "Your friend is stable, but we're going to keep her overnight for observation. We emptied her stomach and she gave us permission to share with you what we found. She has been taking a multitude of drugs and she has been bulimic for several years. She's been mixing prescription drugs with illegal drugs. If she hadn't been with you when she collapsed, she would probably be dead right now."

"Can we see her?" I asked.

"She can only have one visitor tonight, besides the coaches and her parents."

Several of the girls started grumbling.

"Ladies, if you let the pressures of your sport get to you, you could find yourself tempted to take drugs, or to starve yourself or throw up your food just so you can beat that top athlete. But you'll pay a high price for that kind of competitive drive. You may end up here, like your teammate. Or worse."

None of us said a thing. I looked around and noticed that everyone in the room was hanging on the woman's every word. Finally I spoke up. "Doctor, thank you for saving Kirsten's life. And thank you for your speech. We all heard you, and I'm sure your words saved more lives tonight."

"Laurel, you don't need to talk for us," Janet grumbled.

"Laurel," the doctor uttered. "That's the name of the girl Kirsten said she wanted to talk to. Can you come with me, please?"

I felt Janet's eyes boring into the back of my head as I followed the doctor into Kirsten's room. Her parents and the coaches stepped outside after I entered. She asked me to come sit beside her bed. When I did, she took my hand.

"Laurel," she said, her voice hoarse. "The coaches told me what the others were saying to you, and I want you to know this isn't your fault. Yeah, you made it tough for me, but because of you, I'm a better gymnast than I ever thought I could be. I stepped up my game when you were around."

I didn't know what to say, so I just held her hand and let the tears flow.

"I also wanted to thank you for coming into the bathroom when you did and for telling Coach Weslyn what I'd done. I don't think the other girls would have done that. But you didn't look the other way. You held me accountable for my actions."

She looked really tired, so I told her she should just rest.

Kirsten nodded, tears forming in her eyes. "Please tell everyone I'm OK, and tell them to learn from this, because I don't want them to end up like me."

I squeezed her hand and said good night. Then I handed her some tissue and walked out of the room.

Thank You, Lord, I prayed. *Thank You for letting her tell me it wasn't my fault. I'm so thankful that she understands that.*

I got in so late that night that my mother let me stay home from school the next day. When I woke up a little after noon, I immediately got down on my knees beside the bed.

"Lord," I prayed, "I know I shouldn't care what other people say or think of me. As long as I'm doing the right thing, I've tried not to let gossip get under my skin. But even though I'm not trying to, I have been affecting people's lives in a negative way. Coach Milligent is a tyrant sometimes, but I didn't mean for him to get on the other girls just because he sees his grumbling working on me. Please help me talk to him, or help the situation change. I feel so weak inside. Everywhere I turn there's trouble. I need rest and refuge in You. I want to be genuinely happy on the inside, but frankly, I'm not. This latest incident has put out some of my fire for gymnastics. Are You trying to tell me that it's not in Your will for me to continue?"

I didn't feel the Lord saying anything back to me, and I

didn't feel like taking up counsel with my parents or anyone else. Fortunately, my family gave me the space I needed. Mom didn't even say anything about the school team practice I missed.

The Rockdale practice on Saturday morning was cancelled. My parents had a picnic that afternoon with some of the church leaders. Mom asked me to help in the kitchen, even though I wanted no part in the festivities. As soon as my work was done, I retreated back to my room. About an hour later, my dad knocked on my door.

"Laurel, can I come in?"

"Yes, sir," I said respectfully.

He came in and stood by my bed. "I know you've been going through a lot," he said quietly, "and I've been praying for you. I want you to know I'm here for you if you want to talk."

"Thanks, Dad," I replied. "I just don't really have anything to say."

"Well, a friend of yours is here. Maybe a visit would be good for you."

"I'm not up to company," I groaned.

"Why don't you come on down? I think you'll be pleasantly surprised."

I sighed. There was obviously no point in arguing. "OK, I'll be down in a second."

After Dad left my room, I ran a brush through my hair and then went outside. There on the front porch sat my boyfriend. A smile came across my face. When Foster saw me, he stood and gave me a warm embrace.

"I heard you've been going through a lot lately," he said. "I'm sorry I couldn't be there for you." I hugged him tighter. "Are you up to talking about it?"

We sat on the porch swing and I explained every detail. "Coach Milligent wasn't the only one who raised the bar," I said. "I had a big hand in it. And I feel horrible about it."

Foster took my hand. "I feel the same way on the baseball field."

"Really?" I looked into his eyes. They shone with sincerity. "What do you do about it?"

"I just pray," he told me. "I ask God to be the dominant one, not me. When I keep God first, He works everything out."

My soul basked in relief. "Thank you, Foster. I really needed you today. I'm so glad God sent you to me."

Monday started out as just a regular school day. Foster and I were back together. Brittany and I continued our friendship. As the rumors about her died down, she enjoyed her celebrity status again. But Meagan and I still weren't talking. I didn't want her anywhere around until my brothers had settled their differences.

Foster asked me to have lunch with him under a quiet shade tree in the school courtyard. We ate our sack lunches in silence for a few minutes, and then he started asking me some tough questions. "I need to know how you really feel about me," he said. "When I gave you that ring at the dance, you seemed to get upset."

I'd had time to think about my reaction that night, so I shared with him what I'd come up with. "I guess I was scared. Scared of getting my heart broken like I did with Branson."

"But I'm not like Branson," Foster said. "I don't care about trivial things like he does. I care about you."

"I know," I said, twisting the ruby ring on my finger. "But I was still frightened. You know me so well. And yet, for some reason, I still wonder if I can completely trust you."

Foster looked directly into my eyes. "You can trust me, Laurel."

I took a deep breath. "I'm not sure I'm ready to trust anyone again."

Foster started playing with the cellophane wrapped

around his second sandwich. "So, what does all this mean for us? You committed verbally to be my girlfriend, but maybe your heart isn't ready for that." I stared at the trees, their leaves swaying gently in the wind. "You don't have to answer right now," he said. "Just think about it."

"Thanks," I whispered. I was glad he realized he was coming on too strong. Things weren't all that serious between us. We were concentrating on our spiritual issues, and I needed that.

"My little sister, Faigyn, had a talk with me last night," Foster said, tossing his uneaten sandwich back into the paper bag.

"What'd she say?" I asked, grateful for the change in topic.

"She told me she has started liking boys." I could tell Foster felt uncomfortable about his little sister dating. But I couldn't help but laugh. Faigyn was a darling ninth-grade girl who was pretty and sweet and really looked up to me.

"Any boy in particular?" I asked.

"Oh, yes," Foster said, standing. "And you'll never guess who." He grabbed my hand and helped me up. "Luke."

I gulped. "You mean my youngest brother?"

He nodded. "Somehow she convinced my parents to let the four of us go out together."

As I processed this interesting twist, screams suddenly rang out from the lunchroom. Kids poured out the doors and scrambled in all directions.

"What's going on?" Foster asked a boy who rushed past us.

"It's a gun!" he yelled without stopping.

"What?" I said.

"C'mon, Laurel," Foster said, grabbing my hand. "Let's get out of here."

I heard shots. My heart stopped. Surely I must be dreaming.

"Come on!" Foster yanked my hand.

I started to turn, but then I saw Luke standing in the lunchroom doorway. He was staring intently at someone inside the room and inching toward him. I stopped in my tracks. The person he was approaching was pointing a gun right at him!

"No!" I yelled, yanking my hand out of Foster's grip.

"Laurel, this is dangerous."

"Look," I whispered, pointing to Luke.

The gunman was holding a girl by the neck, and it appeared Luke was trying to calm him down. But the guy with the gun didn't seem to want to listen. As he tightened his grip on the hostage's throat, I heard her scream, "Foster!"

I took a closer look at the girl. It was Faigyn!

"Let go of my sister!" Foster yelled, boldly approaching the lunchroom as if he'd lost his mind.

The gunman glared at him and he stopped. Then the crazed guy looked into Faigyn's big brown eyes, which were wide with fright. "Faigyn, I loved you," he murmured. "I wrote you love notes, bought you pretty clothes, and gave you my heart. And now you tell me you want to be with this nerd!" He waved the gun at Luke without taking his eyes off Faigyn. "I'm not gonna let you leave me," he said, his voice growing louder. "I won't let you turn me into a laughing-stock. I'm going to show everyone who is in control!"

The boy turned toward the group of students who had gathered in the courtyard to watch. His face grew pale when he saw police officers making a path through the crowd.

"Don't come any closer," he yelled.

"Preston," one of the cops said, his voice soothing but firm, "put down the gun."

"Don't tell me what to do," Preston growled. He fired a shot into the air. Several students screamed.

Suddenly, my legs went limp and I started falling to the floor. I felt myself slipping into dizziness.

regaining
total control

the sky was spinning, my heart was beating fast, and anxiety was overcoming me, but I knew I had to get a grip. When I opened my eyes, I noticed vomit on my shirt and shoes. The smell of it almost made me throw up again. I wiped my mouth with my hand, then wiped my hand on my shirt.

I closed my eyes and shook my head to try to clear my mind. Had I just heard gunshots?

Heavenly Father, I prayed, *I'm scared. I need Your strength right now. When I open my eyes, what will I see? If Luke, Foster, or Faigyn is dead, I know I can't take it. That's not going to happen, is it, Lord? It just can't!* As I prayed, my heart started to calm and I felt a strange peace wash over my soul. *I know You are listening to me right now. I know You're in control. And I know You will make everything OK. Thank You, Lord.*

My prayer was interrupted by more shots. My eyes flew

open and I stumbled into the lunchroom. The first thing I saw was blood. Everywhere.

"Help me," I heard Foster cry out.

I was glad to hear his voice because it let me know he was still alive. But he was obviously in pain or danger. I wanted to find him, but my eyes refused to focus.

"No!" I heard several unfamiliar voices scream.

"This is horrible," a girl said.

My vision started to clear, and I saw Luke huddled in a ball on the floor of the lunchroom, gripping his right leg. Beside him, I saw Faigyn lying flat on the floor, blood pooled all around her. Near her feet, Foster and the gunman were fighting for control of the pistol. A policeman was trying to pull them apart.

As I started to get up, another officer came between me and the scene of violence, blocking my view. I looked up and saw him staring down at me. "Miss, we need to get you out of here."

"That's my little brother," I said, pointing. "And the girl on the floor is Faigyn McDowell, my boyfriend's sister. I've got to help them."

"We're doing everything we can, Miss," he said in a calming tone. "But we need you to get out of here."

"I'm not leaving without my brother." I sobbed.

"Everything will be OK," he assured me.

A younger-looking police officer interrupted us. "We've got him, sir," he announced. "We've got him!"

I watched as four cops slapped handcuffs on Preston's wrists. He struggled violently. The raging power inside that boy was unbelievable.

"That kid has to be on something," the younger cop muttered.

"No doubt about it," the older one said.

As the officers started dragging Preston away, he turned and spit at Faigyn, who was still lying motionless on the floor. I wondered if she was even alive.

I prayed for Preston's soul. His rage had no mercy. He

needed Christ. No guy should ever get so angry at a girl that he felt a need to get revenge in such a dramatic way.

As the cops dragged Preston toward a police cruiser in the school parking lot, Preston yelled profanities at Faigyn and Luke. Finally they tucked him into the backseat and drove away.

The principal and several teachers started clearing the gawking crowds, encouraging everyone to go to their classes. I ran to Luke, who was still huddled on the floor, his eyes squeezed shut. "Luke, are you OK?" I asked frantically.

"Check on Faigyn," he groaned, grasping his right foot.

I looked down. A bullet had left a ragged hole in his tennis shoe, and blood was spilling out. "Don't worry about her right now, Luke. You've got to get to the hospital." I looked around and saw paramedics arriving. "Right here!" I called to one of them. "This is my brother. He was shot in the foot."

"OK, ma'am," he said, rushing toward us. "We've got him."

I moved out of the way. As the paramedic examined Luke, I looked around and saw Foster sitting on the ground, rocking Faigyn in his arms. Two paramedics were checking her vital signs as he held her. Seeing that my brother was being well taken care of, I hurried over to my boyfriend.

He was sobbing, tears drenching his face. "Laurel," he cried, his voice husky, "I don't know if she's OK or not."

I knelt beside him and held his head to my chest.

One of the paramedics looked up at us. "She was shot in the arm, and the fall knocked her unconscious. But she's going to be all right."

They gently convinced Foster to release his sister, and they placed her on a gurney. As they rolled her to a waiting ambulance, I noticed the police had started questioning witnesses.

Foster and I stood there, staring at the scene around us. Neither of us could speak a word. Foster took me in his arms and we wept. Though the situation was under control, our emotions weren't. But we were thankful that God had gotten us through it and that we had each other to lean on.

As Foster and I walked out of the lunchroom, I felt emotionally drained. I knew I probably looked like a Mack truck had hit me. Our friends rushed up to us, and we got separated in the crowd.

The first person I saw was Meagan. She squeezed me so tight I could barely breathe. "Laurel," she cried, "I'm so happy to see you. I'm glad you're OK."

Suddenly, forgiving Meagan was easy. She hadn't meant to cause trouble by coming between my two brothers. I returned her embrace without a second thought. "I am so glad to see you," I blubbered.

That gunman could have taken any of our lives. Mine. Meagan's. Foster's. Certainly Luke's or Faigyn's. But the Lord had helped us through this terrible ordeal.

As Meagan and I cried on each other's shoulders, I noticed Brittany standing beside her. I released one arm and drew her into our hug.

"Life is so precious," she said. "I just want you to know that I love you."

Meagan and I assured Brittany that we loved her too.

"And this guy here was really worried about you," Brittany added as she pulled Branson from behind her.

I looked into his eyes and saw deep concern. Brittany and Meagan stepped away so Branson could give me a hug. When he wrapped his arms around me, he picked me up and spun me around like he had done many times before. But this time he held my head close to his chest, as if I were precious cargo he never wanted to let go. When I was dating him, he had never shown me so much affection. There was no doubting what he felt for me. His eyes revealed what his mouth refrained from saying.

"I'm all right, Branson," I said when he put me down. "I'm fragile, but I'm in one piece. Luke is OK too."

"Looks like we're both going to be fine," he responded with a smile.

"What do you mean?"

"My last test came back negative," he announced, his smile growing broader. "The doctors feel pretty confident that I'm out of danger."

"That's great news!" I looked around and saw that my friends had left us alone. "Have you told Brittany?"

"Not yet. I know she'll be happy for me, but I don't think this is the right time. I don't want to rub it in her face."

"I understand," I told him. "You're probably right."

Foster found his way back to me. When Branson saw him, he reached out and shook Foster's hand. "Thank you for saving Laurel's life," he said. Foster looked flustered. It was a weird exchange, but it made me appreciate both of them.

"My pleasure," Foster finally said.

As my boyfriend led me through the crowd, I waved good-bye to Branson. Part of me hated to leave him because I could tell he wanted to celebrate the test results with me. It was nice to see him changed, but he had changed too late. I was where I needed to be. I was extremely happy being Foster McDowell's girlfriend.

Foster pulled me toward the student parking lot. "The principal told me my parents went to the hospital to see Faigyn, and your parents are waiting here for us. We've got to find them."

We searched the crowded mass of cars and people. Finally, I heard my mother call my name. "Mom!" I called back.

When we found each other, she checked my whole body to make sure I was really all right.

"I'm OK, Mom," I assured her. "You guys didn't have to wait for me. You could have gone with Luke to the hospital."

"We talked to him before the paramedics took him away," my father said. "The McDowells promised they'd check on him when they got to the hospital. Lance and Liam rode in the ambulance with him." Dad turned to Foster. "I heard about what you did, Son," he said, placing his arm on Foster's shoulder. "It was very brave, but also extremely dangerous. You and other people could have been killed."

"I know, sir," Foster said. "But when I saw Faigyn, something came over me."

"Mom," I asked, "did anyone find out what was wrong with Preston?"

My father's face turned angry. "The police said he was on some kind of narcotics."

I threw my arms around my dad's neck. "It's all over now," I said, trying to comfort him.

But when I pulled back, his face was still red. "I send you guys to school to get an education, and now we have to worry about you coming home alive. What is this world coming to?"

I suddenly thought about Liam and Lance. Dad had said they'd ridden to the hospital together. I wondered how they were feeling about each other. "Hey, let's get going to the hospital."

As we all piled into the family van, I looked up toward heaven and whispered, "Thank You, Lord. Thank You."

Foster crawled into the backseat next to me. "So, what was Branson talking to you about?" he asked.

"Nothing," I assured him. "He was just happy to see that I was all right."

"Yeah, I could tell that." He took my hand. "It was strange how he thanked me for saving your life. It was kind of like he still considers you his girlfriend."

I rolled my eyes. "Don't go getting jealous on me. I've had a rough day."

My parents were talking up front so they weren't listening to my conversation with Foster. However, this was not the time or place for us to be having this conversation.

"So, my suspicion isn't completely unfounded," Foster said. "You still care for him."

I glared at Foster. "Yes, I still care for him. So what?"

My dad peeked at us through the rearview mirror. "Are you guys OK back there?" he asked.

"We're fine," I said. Then I turned my back to Foster and stared out the window.

Foster was really irritating me, but I wasn't about to make a big deal out of it in front of my father. I was concerned about Luke, and Foster should have been concerned about Faigyn, yet here he was grilling me.

I focused my thoughts on the gunman, Preston. I remembered being really angry when Brittany and Branson got together, but I'd never wanted them dead! What could possibly have pushed this guy over the edge?

———————

"Thanks for letting me crash here for a couple of nights, Robyn," I said as I unpacked my suitcase. "With my grandparents staying at my house, the place is kind of crowded."

"Sure, no problem," Robyn said, rearranging the contents of her dresser to clear out a drawer for me. "We haven't been able to hang out as much lately as we used to."

"Yeah, I miss you too," I said.

Robyn's face grew serious. "How's your brother?"

"He's OK. The bullet just grazed the top of his foot. Didn't hit any bones or tendons or muscles or anything. He's supposed to stay in bed for about a week, but he'll be running around in no time."

"I'm glad to hear that," she said. "And what about Foster's sister?"

"Faigyn had to stay at the hospital overnight because of the concussion. But she's home now, with a cast on her arm. The bullet nicked her humerus." I remembered how much

Branson had suffered with the cast on his arm, especially toward the end when it started itching. But Faigyn had a lot more emotional trauma connected with her broken armbone than he'd had with his football injury. That would take a lot longer to heal.

As I put my stuff away, I listened to the song Robyn had playing on the CD. A man was singing gospel in a sultry voice. His lyrics expressed everything I was feeling. I started asking myself the same questions the artist was singing. *What should I do when I've done everything I can think of for my friends, but they just turn their backs on me? When guilt from my past fills me with shame, what can I do?* As the singer belted out the answer, my heart sang along. I knew that all I needed to do was stand and watch the Lord work everything out. I just had to keep standing.

"Who is this?" I asked as I turned up the volume.

"Donnie McClurkin," Robyn said, pulling out some empty hangers from her closet. "That song's called 'Stand.' " She started singing along.

I stood there with my clothes draped over my arm, totally blown away by Robyn's beautiful alto voice. "I didn't know you could sing so great!"

She shrugged. "Yeah, I sing a little."

"You should have Mrs. Moreland give you some solos."

I played the song three more times, and by the end of the third time, I was singing along with Robyn. We made a great duet.

"You've been holding out on me too," she said. "Your voice is gorgeous. I wish I could sing soprano. Let's do some more stuff together." Before I could say yes or no, she started belting out "Amazing Grace." I joined in right away, and we sang all the verses. As I thought about how God had helped me through the shooting, I sang from my heart. As we held the last note, my eyes welled with tears.

"You've got soul in your voice, girl," Robyn said.

"Thanks. It's easy to sing beautifully when you think

about the words and about all the wonderful grace God gives us so freely."

Before we could start another song, Robyn's mother entered the room. "Laurel," she said, "Robyn told me about what happened at school. Are you OK?"

I nodded. "Yeah, I'm getting through it."

"You know, you girls sounded wonderful singing together."

"Thanks, Mrs. Williams," I said, blushing a little.

She started to leave, then turned back. "Oh, I almost forgot. I was just talking to my friend Robin the other day—"

"Robin Jones Gunn?" I guessed.

"Yes." She smiled. "I know how much you like her books. Well, we're getting together with her this summer, and I thought you might want to come along and meet her."

My eyes opened wide. "You name the time and the place, and I'll be there."

Mrs. Williams chuckled. "I thought you might say that."

"I finished the latest book in her Sierra Jensen series. And I already wish I had something else of hers to read."

Robyn nudged me. "You could read my mom's latest book. Her copies of it just came in the mail the other day."

I remembered the manuscript Mrs. Williams had asked me to read for her. It was different from Robin Jones Gunn's books, mostly because the main character was a black girl. But I really liked the story. And I especially enjoyed offering my ideas and input on what life is like for today's teens. "Is this the one I read for you a few months ago?" I asked.

Robyn and her mom laughed. "It takes a lot more than a few months to get a book published," my friend informed me.

"The manuscript you read for me is going to be the sequel to the one that just got published," Mrs. Williams explained.

"OK," I said eagerly. "Where can I buy one and how much do they cost?"

"Oh, you don't have to pay for them," Robyn's mom said. "I'll be happy to give you an autographed copy."

"That'd be great!"

As she started to leave again, I thanked her for letting me stay at her house.

"No problem." She smiled. "You're a good influence on Robyn."

She told us good night, and Robyn and I spent the rest of the night talking. Robyn was becoming a great friend and a calming diversion from my crazy world.

When Mom drove me to my next gymnastics practice at Rockdale on Thursday, instead of just dropping me off, she parked the car.

"What are you doing?" I asked.

"We have a parent meeting," she told me as she got out.

As we approached the gym, the looks on the parents' faces told me this was going to be a very serious meeting. When we walked inside, there were chairs set up in rows facing a small podium. Mom and I sat down. I looked around for Coach Milligent and saw him seated on the far end of the front row, his eyes focused on the gym floor.

Betty Wells, Kirsten's mom, stood behind the podium. One by one, she invited five of the gymnasts to come up and explain how afraid they were of Coach Milligent and how they felt about his tough tactics.

After the last girl sat down, Mrs. Wells addressed the coach directly. "We all feel that you're putting too much pressure on these girls. They are not slaves. None of us was aware of this treatment until the incident with Kirsten. But now, several of the parents here have agreed that if you don't back down, they are going to pull their daughters from the team until a new coach can be found."

Mom leaned over and whispered in my ear, "Is that how you feel too?"

I shrugged. "I'm used to his gruffness. It actually helps me perform better. I don't want him gone."

Mrs. Wells called for a show of hands. Mom and I kept ours in our laps. But two-thirds of the team indicated that they wanted Coach Milligent gone.

Finally, the coach walked up to the podium, and Mrs. Wells took a seat. I'd never seen him look so dejected. "I'm very sorry that you feel this way," he said. "I only want what's best for you girls." He cleared his throat. "I have discussed this matter with Assistant Coach Weslyn. She has agreed to take over my position, with the condition that I stay on as assistant coach."

After a few moments of mumbling, Mrs. Wells called for another vote. I didn't know whether to raise my hand or not. But enough people did, so the proposition was accepted.

"I hope the rest of your season goes well," Coach Milligent said, then he left the room with his shoulders slumped.

The girls who had voted for him to leave stood and started hugging each other. Some of them even cheered. I was appalled. "Mom, this doesn't seem right."

"I know, honey," she said. "But it will work out. Remember, God is still in control."

I thanked her with a hug. "Mom, I want to go to church with you tonight." Normally, we didn't have services on Thursday nights, but Dad had prepared a special sermon for those who'd been affected by the shooting incident at school.

An hour later we were sitting in the sanctuary listening to my dad preach a powerful sermon. Right there in the pulpit, he announced to the congregation, "This past week, I believed I had failed as a father." The congregation murmured for a moment. "But then I said a prayer for forgiveness and guidance. And God gave me hope."

He took a deep breath, then went on. "The Lord showed me that no matter what I do as a parent, or how much I wish I could protect my children, I can't always keep them out of harm's way. As I saw my youngest son being carried from school on a stretcher because he was shot by another student, I wanted to do something drastic. I wanted to mete out judgment to the slayer. I didn't know how I could allow any of my children to go to school again."

More murmurs indicated that most of the folks in the congregation agreed with my dad. "But God let me see that they are not really my children. They're His. I have to learn to trust the Lord with everything, including my children. When life gets crazy, we've got to remember who is on the throne and who is in control. We have to let the Lord have a place in everything that happens in our lives. Only when we are willing to follow will He direct our paths. We need to give the power back to the one who can handle it."

Someone in the back hollered out, "Amen!"

"If you want to see a change in your life," my father continued, "you need to get on your knees and ask the heavenly Father to start regaining total control."

fooling
with trouble

i know it's late," Robyn said to me on the phone that night after church. "I promise I won't keep you long."

I sat up in my bed. "Are you OK? You sound like you've been crying."

"You sound like you're asleep. I'll just talk to you tomorrow."

"No, that's OK. I was about to go to sleep, but I'm still awake. What's wrong?"

"Well," she said, still hesitating. "You know how happy I've been that Jackson and I are back together, right?"

"Yeah."

"And he's been really nice to me and everything."

"That's good," I said, wishing she'd get to her point but willing to let her tell me at her own pace. There was obviously something really bothering her.

"Well, he came over today. At first we were just talking and—"

"Robyn," I whined, remembering the drama she'd gone through with this boy. Robyn had forgiven him for cheating on her and for convincing her to take their relationship too far. When she found out she was pregnant, she'd really fallen apart. Then, after she aborted the baby, she became almost suicidal. Somehow, she had been able to put all that behind her and take him back. But I'd been skeptical about how long it would be before he returned to his old ways. "Please tell me nothing happened," I said.

"You know how sexy he is, girl," she said defensively.

"What's that supposed to mean?"

"Laurel, I couldn't stop him. I know I should have, but I couldn't help it. I felt terrible after. When it was over, I was sure he would leave and go back to the way he used to be. But he didn't. He was attentive when I cried, and he said he was sorry. He told me he wanted me so bad that he couldn't help himself. Laurel, we were connecting."

A million warning lights flashed through my mind, but I couldn't think of a single thing to say to her. I couldn't believe she'd allowed this to happen again!

Her voice sounded sad. "Then I realized that I didn't regret it at all. I was really glad we'd done it because it brought us so much closer." She paused. "The Lord hates me, huh?"

At that point I couldn't even answer her. I was sure the Lord didn't hate her, but I was beginning to have severe doubts about her salvation. If she had no power over sin and no real desire to please God instead of just pleasing herself, then there was something wrong. There was more going on here than just a physical relationship with Jackson Reid.

"How could you?" I asked, practically in tears myself.

"I don't know," she cried. "It's like Jackson is a drug. I thought I was fine, and then—"

"Robyn, you're playing with danger."

"I know. That's why I needed to talk to you. Laurel, I understand that what I did was wrong. But why did it feel so right?"

I didn't know what to say to Robyn. I knew the Lord led her to me for some reason, but why? What was I supposed to say?

As I tried to formulate an answer for her, my dad peeked in on me. "Laurel, don't you think it's a little late to be on the phone on a school night?"

"Yeah, Dad. I'm getting off now." He nodded and left. "You heard that, right?" I asked Robyn.

"Yeah, you have to go," she said sadly.

"I'll talk to you tomorrow, OK?"

She said, "OK," but she didn't sound OK.

After hanging up the phone, I fell to my knees and prayed. "Lord, sometimes I just don't understand why people do the things they do. But I know You must feel the same way about me sometimes. Please convict Robyn of her sin and show her that You are standing beside her, with open arms, ready to forgive her when she repents. Giving in to physical temptation seems to be a continual struggle for her, Lord. And now she's right back in the saddle with that jerk. Help her to see what a dangerous game she's playing."

I tossed and turned all night, asking myself why people got so caught up with the flesh. When I realized I wouldn't come up with any answers any time soon, I gave up and fell into a less-than-perfect slumber.

The next morning, as Robyn and I walked to our classes together, she stopped suddenly and turned to face me. "Quit looking at me that way," she said.

"What way?" I asked.

"You know full well that you've been giving me a glare of disapproval since the moment you saw me this morning."

She was right, and I felt really bad about it. "Robyn, can I ask you something?"

"Sure."

"How do you feel today?"

She leaned against the wall of lockers and thought about it. "The same as before, I guess. I'm bummed out because I

couldn't hold out. But it felt good being with Jackson again."
When she saw the disappointed look in my eyes, she added,
"I know you've got more willpower than I do. But don't you
just sometimes want to be with Foster completely?"

"Robyn!"

"What? I thought we were being honest here."

I adjusted the schoolbooks in my arms. Suddenly they
felt heavy and awkward. "Sure, I've felt that way before. But
you've got to ask God for strength. And I thought that was
what you were doing."

She sighed. "I thought I was too. But I just couldn't keep
it up."

We started walking again. "So, is this going to be a one-
time mistake or an everyday thing?" I asked.

"I haven't thought that far ahead."

"What if you get pregnant again?" I asked. "Have you
thought about that?"

"He wore protection," Robyn argued.

I shook my head. "I don't want to help you figure out
how to be *safe,*" I said, emphasizing the last word with sar-
casm. "That's not the issue here. The question is, does God
have control in your life? It seems you've been running
things in your life so far. Last time you did that, you aborted
your baby."

I could tell by the look on her face that I'd touched a
part of her that still hurt deeply. But that look quickly disappeared and was replaced by a cold glare. "Are you judging
me?" she asked.

"No," I said, wanting to be sensitive to her feelings, but
also knowing I needed to be firm on this, for her sake. "But
maybe you should judge yourself. I care about you, Robyn.
After you got the abortion, you were hurting so bad, it
broke my heart. And now you're walking down the same
road again. Are you suddenly over all the pain that caused
you?"

"No," she said softly. "I'll never be over it. I'll always remember that day."

I took her hand. "Then why are you acting like you'll never be in that position again?"

"I don't know," she whispered.

"Look," I added, "it's not just the potential for getting pregnant that bothers me. It's the fact that you're basically saying that pleasing your flesh is more important than pleasing your spirit and pleasing the Lord. You're playing with fire here, and I don't want to see you get burned."

At that moment, the bell rang. "I've got to get to class," Robyn said, then took off. She was clearly irritated by what I had said, but I wasn't going to apologize. She needed to hear the words I'd said to her, and I was glad I said them because it was like the words had flowed through me straight from heaven.

I knew physical desire was hard to turn down, but I also knew that God could put out that fire. Physical pleasure only lasts for a moment. But the Lord can give a person a fire that lasts a lifetime . . . a new life full of joy and dependence on Him to meet every need. That's what I wanted Robyn to have. That's what I wanted her to think about. And that was why I was glad I told her.

"I'm tired of studying. Let's take a break." Meagan tossed her physics book onto my bed and indulged herself in an exaggerated stretch.

"How can you be tired?" I asked. "We only started thirty minutes ago. We have midterms coming up and I want to be prepared." I'd been studying almost nonstop for a week. When Meagan asked if I'd help her get ready for the physics test, I thought it would be a good way to start breaking the ice between us. But it soon became obvious that studying wasn't really the first thing on her mind.

"Look, Meagan," I said, "I'd really like to exempt all of

my exams at the end of the year, and the only way I can do that is if I keep up my grades now. This test counts for 20 percent of our grade, girl."

"I know," she whined, "but let's just take a small break, OK? Maybe get something to drink."

"I'm not thirsty," I said, returning my attention to the textbook. "You can get something if you want."

"OK," she said, hopping off my bed. "I'll bring you back some water."

I wasn't sure whether Meagan knew all the information she needed for the tests, or if getting a good grade wasn't that high on her priority list, but whatever was going on with her, I was determined not to let it get me off track. However, when ten minutes passed and she still hadn't come back, I knew something was up. Then it dawned on me that she still had problems with my brothers. When I wandered to the kitchen and heard Liam's upset voice, I knew I had made the wrong decision by letting her come over. I stopped just outside the kitchen doorway and listened.

"So, what are you trying to do, Meagan?" I heard my oldest younger brother say. "Date Luke now?"

"No," she said. "I was just trying to make sure—"

"Save it. You've already been with one of my brothers."

"Let me explain," Meagan begged.

"Just get out of my way!"

"Hey," I heard my youngest brother, Luke, interject. "Why are you being so nasty to her?"

"Please just listen to me, Liam," Meagan pleaded.

"You've got nothing to say that I want to hear," Liam growled.

"How can you be so cold?" she cried.

I couldn't wait quietly on the outside any longer. This conversation was going nowhere and someone was about to get really hurt. I knew Liam well enough to know that he wasn't going to give my friend the comfort she so desperately needed. "Meagan," I said as I walked into the kitchen, "come on. Let's go back and study."

With sad puppy-dog eyes she stared at Liam, but he stood firm. With a deep sob, she dashed past me toward my room.

Before I could follow her, Liam stepped up to me with a glare of disapproval. "How dare you bring her into this house?" he said. "I can't even sleep in my own room because Lance and I aren't talking to each other, and it's all because of that girl. I thought you were mad at her too. You told me how important reconciliation between me and Lance is, yet you bring her over here before we've had a chance to settle things."

"We're studying for a test," I said lamely.

"News flash," he said sarcastically. "Isn't there a place called the library? I hear some people actually study for tests there."

"Hey," I said defensively, "a lot of stuff has happened to me lately. Luke and I could have been killed at school the other day. And when that happened, I learned something. You can't live your life being mad at people. You have to forgive them and move on. I know you're angry with Meagan, but clearly she still cares for you. Those were not fake tears in her eyes. Can't you see she's broken inside?"

He flipped on the tap and filled his glass with water. "Look," he said, "even if we got things straightened out, sooner or later she'd go running back to Lance. Then I'd get my heart broken all over again. I will not be a sucker twice!" He stormed out of the kitchen with his glass of water.

I couldn't imagine what had brought Liam to this place of sheer anger. He had the biggest Christian heart I knew, and now he was being brutally negative. Had Meagan hurt him that badly? Or was something else going on with him?

"Liam's pretty upset, huh?" Luke said, sitting at the kitchen table with a bag of potato chips.

"Yeah," I agreed. Not wanting to get into it at the moment, I sat down with him and asked, "But how have you been doing?"

"Fine," he said with a sweet smile. "I've forgiven Preston," he added. "I guess that's what makes it difficult to understand why Liam can't forgive Meagan. Sure, granting forgiveness to someone who has hurt you is difficult. But I've asked God to give me a heart that's not so hard in that area."

"Have you talked to Faigyn lately?" I asked. "Do you know how she's doing?"

Luke nodded. "She can hardly sleep at night." He took a deep breath. "Just knowing how this whole thing is affecting her makes me really angry." He shifted in his seat. "And that anger scares me . . . a lot."

"Scares you?" I asked.

"Yeah. It doesn't seem right to have feelings for someone that are so strong that if you lose them, you change."

"I don't follow you."

"Look at Liam," Luke said. "He was perfectly happy with Meagan, and then she starts messing with Lance, and now Liam's acting crazy. And Preston was a normal guy until Faigyn broke up with him. I like Faigyn so much, I was willing to lose my life for her. But then I asked myself why. I don't want to care for anyone that much. I'm in the ninth grade, for goodness' sake!"

"What you did was heroic, Luke," I told him. "But maybe it wasn't a great romantic love for Faigyn that made you willing to risk your life for her. I think you just wanted to do the right thing—the Christian thing."

"You think so?"

I smiled. "Don't beat yourself up just because you were there for her."

Luke popped a potato chip into his mouth. "Faigyn is mad at me," he said, crunching the chip.

"Why?" I asked.

"Because I'm not as mad at Preston as she is."

"That's ridiculous."

"I just don't want a girl to dictate my thoughts," Luke said. "I want my direction to come only from heaven."

"You're so smart, Luke," I said as I gripped his face with both of my hands. "I'll remember that day at school forever."

"Do you feel angry about what happened?"

"I don't know," I answered honestly. "I've pretty much just tried to put it out of my mind. But hearing you talk about forgiveness lets me know that I need to do the same thing." I patted his hand. "Keep being an example, Luke. You may be the youngest in our family, but you're definitely the wisest."

He beamed at me. "Thanks for listening, Sis."

"Thanks for sharing," I said. "Now, I really should get back to Meagan."

"Tell her to hang in there," he counseled.

"I will." I got up and started for the door.

Luke hopped to the cupboard to put away the bag of chips. "Hey," I said, wagging a finger at him, "you stop jumping around on that foot. Doctor said you were supposed to stay in bed."

"I'm tired of that room," he said, closing the cupboard door. "Lance and Liam are driving me crazy."

I laughed with him, then hurried up to my bedroom. When I opened the door, I saw Meagan balled up on the floor, crying. I rushed over and knelt beside her. "Don't worry, Meagan," I said, stroking her shoulder. "Liam will come around. You've just got to give him some time."

"I really do care for him, Laurel," she sobbed. "Why does he hate me so much?"

"Maybe because you kissed Lance?" I suggested gently.

"But that's all that happened," she said.

"Is it really?" I asked.

She looked up, her face wet with tears. "Yes!"

"Well, let me talk to him," I said. "Maybe I can straighten some of this out. In the meantime, why don't you go on home and get some rest?"

She sniffled. "We didn't even get to study."

I chuckled. "You didn't seem too concerned about physics earlier."

"I know," she said, blowing her nose with a tissue. "I was thinking too much about Liam to concentrate on school-work."

"Just pray about it," I said, helping her up off the floor. "Everything's going to work out."

"Are you sure?" she asked, her red eyes filled with un-certainty.

I wasn't really sure if Liam would ever come around, but just to comfort her, I said, "Yeah, I'm sure."

After Meagan left, I thought of how much I hated being in the middle of all this drama. *Lord, help!* I prayed.

As I sat in the theater on Monday night, watching a movie I'd been waiting to see for a month, I couldn't believe what I was doing. I'd asked Foster to see the film with me, but he wasn't too enthused about it. So I didn't feel very guilty about saying yes when Branson asked me to see it with him.

I looked at my ex-boyfriend, sitting there next to me in the dark theater. *What is wrong with me?* I wondered as I watched him eat a handful of popcorn.

That morning, Foster had asked me if I was going to his baseball game after school. Very sincerely, I told him I had other plans. I just didn't tell him what those plans were.

"I know you, Laurel," he'd said. "Monday is April Fool's Day. You're just playing around, aren't you? I bet you're gonna show up anyway to cheer me on." I hadn't even an-swered him.

But knowing that Foster was finishing up his game while I was at the movies with my ex was starting to make me feel bad.

Branson turned to me. "You're supposed to be watching the movie, not me," he whispered.

"Oh, I'm sorry," I said, embarrassed.

The couple in front of us turned around and asked us to be quiet. I stopped talking but couldn't concentrate on the images on the screen. My seat felt really uncomfortable for some reason, and I kept fidgeting.

"Are you OK?" Branson asked quietly.

"Yeah," I said. "I'm just not feeling good."

"You wanna leave?"

"No, I'll be fine."

But as the minutes passed, I started feeling even more uncomfortable. Was I sending wrong messages to Branson? Did he think I would ever want to get back with him? I sure hoped not.

I also felt bad about not telling Foster what my plans were. If he found out I'd gone to the movies with my ex-boyfriend, would he be angry enough to break off our relationship? If Foster went out innocently with a friend, would I be angry?

When the credits started rolling and the lights came up, Branson and I stayed in our seats waiting for the crowd to thin out. It was something we'd always done when we were dating.

"I'm glad you came here with me tonight," he said. "It makes me realize we still have a chance. I know you're with Foster, but you must still feel something for me or you wouldn't be here."

"You're reading way too much into this," I said. "It's just a movie."

"No, I think I'm right. You still care about me."

I stood and headed for the aisle. Branson rose, too, and I felt his hand on my lower back. It felt way better than I wanted it to.

When we got to the lobby, he asked, "Do you want to get something to eat?"

"No, but I need to go to the restroom," I told him.

"I'll wait right here."

As soon as I opened the bathroom door, I saw Robyn. I suddenly felt really embarrassed. I wanted to turn around before she saw me, but it was too late.

"Laurel, hey! I didn't know you were going to the movies tonight." We hadn't talked since the day I'd gotten on her case about Jackson Reid.

"Sorry," I said as I walked into an open stall. "Gotta go."

"I'll wait for you. I want to say hi to Foster."

"No," I said, hesitating in the doorway. "I mean, you don't have to wait. I'm sure you and Jackson have big plans."

She eyed me suspiciously. "Something's up with you, Laurel. You don't even like Jackson, and I'm sure you wouldn't approve of our plans. Go ahead and use the bathroom. I'll wait."

I stayed in the stall for a long time, hoping she'd leave. But when I finally came out she was still standing there, leaning against the wall near the paper towel dispenser. I took my time washing and drying my hands, then said, "I've got something to tell you."

"What?" she asked as we walked out of the bathroom.

Immediately Branson walked up to us. "Hey, Robyn. Who are you here with?"

"I'm with Jackson. Who did you come with?"

He blinked. "Laurel. She didn't tell you?" He smirked. "Oh, you thought she was here with Choir Boy."

"We're just seeing the same movie," I said, playing it down to my friend.

"Wait here a second, Branson," Robyn said. "We'll be right back." She pulled me to a corner. "What are you doing here with him?" she railed. "And you were lecturing me about what's right and wrong? You're in a relationship with another guy and you're here with your ex!"

"We just came to see a movie," I argued. "He's taking me home right now." At the sound of familiar laughter, I turned around. Jackson and Branson were exchanging laughs.

I started to walk toward them, but Robyn grabbed my arm. "You'd better call me tomorrow and give me the 411," she said with a smile.

"I will," I said. We joined the guys, and after a quick hello and good-bye to Jackson, Branson and I took off. "You be good," I whispered to Robyn.

"Ditto," she said to me.

As Branson drove me home, he said, "You didn't want her to see us together, did you?" He grinned. "If we were just friends, it wouldn't be a big deal."

"But people don't understand that, Branson."

The grin suddenly disappeared from his lips and his voice. "Oh, my gosh," he said, "we're going to have to pull over."

"Why?" I asked, looking behind us to see if there was a police vehicle there.

"I'm out of gas," he said.

"What?"

As he pulled his blue Camaro to the curb, my heart started racing. We were only four miles from my house, but there was nothing along the road besides trees. Being stuck in the woods with Branson was not a good thing.

"I don't have a gas can in the car," he said in a seductive voice. Then he reached over and tried to kiss me. Pulling away from him, I said, "Then we'll just have to walk to my house and get a gas can from there."

As I started to open my car door, Branson said, "April Fool's! I have gas. I just wanted to spend some time with you."

"This isn't funny," I said. "Please take me home."

Branson looked downcast, but he started the car again and headed for my house. As we turned onto my street, I saw a car in my driveway that I did not want to see. It was Foster's midnight blue Toyota Celica. I looked closer and saw that Foster was standing on the porch talking with Liam.

"Stop!" I hollered. "You can let me out right here."

"No way," Branson argued. "I can drop you off at your house."

"Really, it's OK."

"Oh," he said, catching on. "There's someone at your house, and you don't want them to see you with me."

Ignoring my wishes, Branson pulled right up to the curb in front of my house. I wanted to hit him, but I knew I'd brought this whole thing on myself. Stuff was about to get crazy, but that's what I deserved for fooling with trouble.

smoking
on vacation

foster started fuming when he saw Branson pull up to the curb. I felt so stupid I couldn't even bring myself to get out of the car. I hadn't thought of our night at the movies as a date, but I guess that's what it was. Foster had wanted me to support him at his baseball game, but I chose to sit in a movie theater with my ex-boyfriend. If I could do it all over again, I would make a different choice. But that wasn't an option. I had to get out of the car, walk up to the porch, and face my boyfriend. I could only hope the chord between Foster and me would be soft and smooth, not hard and rocky.

"Want me to walk you in?" Branson teased.

"No," I grumbled, opening the car door. "You've done enough already."

"Hey, I wonder if Lance is home." I turned around and saw Branson checking out the house. "I'd like to talk to him about some stuff." He turned to me. "You don't have a problem with that, do you? Your parents are here this time, so it's OK for me to come in, right?"

"Why are you trying to cause me problems?" I asked, seething with anger. "You can see my boyfriend is standing right there on the porch."

He shook his head. "I thought you said we were friends. But obviously you don't even want me to be here."

"I don't need you to get all mad at me over this, Branson. If you want to take it that way, then you really do need to leave. I'll tell Lance you said hello."

I got out of the car and slammed the door shut, then walked toward my house without a backward glance. I heard Branson peel out down the street.

I approached Foster, hoping he would be understanding and give me another chance. *What am I going to say to him?* I wondered as I walked. *Maybe I shouldn't say anything until he cools down.*

The closer I got to the front door, the more I wanted to take off running in the opposite direction. When I finally stepped onto the porch, Foster's eyes were full of disappointment and sorrow, which made me feel ten times worse.

Liam, on the other hand, leaned on the porch railing giving me hate stares. He didn't even have the courtesy to give my boyfriend and me some privacy. I knew he and Foster were best friends, but this was between the two of us. I shot my brother a look that told him to leave. He gave me one back that told me he wasn't going anywhere.

"Why?" Foster uttered softly, looking dejected. He wasn't coming down hard on me, like I'd expected. But this response was worse. His sensitiveness struck my heart like a lightning bolt.

I couldn't think of anything to say. As I watched Foster fighting back tears, I knew there was nothing I could do to get myself out of this hot water. So I said the only thing I could say. "I'm sorry, Foster." I grabbed both of his hands. "Branson and I went to a movie together, but only as friends. It wasn't a date. We just wanted to see the same movie. But all I could think about the whole time was you and your baseball game."

"You looked pretty surprised to see me," he said, his voice weak.

"No, I was happy to see you." I placed my hands on his cheeks.

"It sure took you a while to get out of the car," he said, pulling away.

I sighed. "I knew it would be awkward to explain all of this. But I really am happy to see you."

"Don't try to pacify me," he said, then he stomped down the porch steps.

"Foster, wait! I want to talk."

He stopped at the bottom of the stairs and turned. "Laurel, I need some time to think." He turned toward my brother. "Good night, Liam. Thanks for keeping me company, man."

"Sure," my brother said. "See ya."

Foster got into his car and drove away. All I could do was stare at him. My only hope was that this would not be the last time his car would grace my driveway.

"You should have tried out for the school play," Liam said.

I turned to face him. "What are you talking about?"

"With the great acting you just did for Foster, you would have gotten the lead role."

"I wasn't acting, Liam," I said, tearing up.

"Yeah, whatever, Laurel. You aren't sorry. You and your little friends are never sorry until you get caught."

"Don't even say that," I yelled.

"Why not? You know it's true. You and Meagan are just alike when it comes to men."

"Men?" I rolled my eyes. "Please!"

"Are you trying to put me down now? Like you put Foster down? Do you think Branson's a big man? Is he the only one who can satisfy you?"

I glared at him, so angry I couldn't move or say anything.

"If things are so innocent between you two," Liam went on, "why didn't you tell Foster what you were going to do in the first place? He's a good guy, and if you don't like him, then tell him. Don't humiliate him. Don't be phony and lie to his face."

"I wasn't lying," I argued. "I didn't mean to hurt Foster. Why are you taking this so personal anyway? This is between Foster and me. Why are you on his side?"

"Because I know how he feels," Liam said. "He could barely hold up. I know what it's like to feel strongly for a girl and to think she cares about you, and then see her with another guy. You can't believe God is at all pleased with the way you're misleading Foster." Without giving me another chance to speak up for myself, Liam went inside. The screen door slammed behind him. I stood on the porch alone for a few more minutes, then followed him in.

As I trudged up to my room, I knew in my heart that Liam was right.

The next week went by fast. I spent most of it studying for midterms and reading God's Word. I reflected on Liam's questions, concerns, and comments and I tried to get closer to the Lord. I asked Him to reveal to me what in the world was going on with my brain. Why was I so unsatisfied with a good guy? As much as I tried to doubt Liam's attack on my character, I knew he was right. In my eyes, Branson was a bad boy and part of me liked playing with fire. There was definitely a struggle going on within, because I liked spending time with Branson just as much as I wanted to stroll on the safe side with Foster.

But Foster would not settle for 50 percent of my attention. He had proven that by not calling me all week. I tried phoning him on Saturday, but his sister gave me the runaround. I ended up asking her questions for almost thirty minutes: Had she gotten over the shooting? Was she sleeping well? Had her arm healed?

A simple "no" was her answer every time.

Finally I asked her if she would let me pray with her. Again she said no.

I really wanted to talk to Foster. I had to let him know that he needed to be there for his sister. When he didn't return my call, I realized he didn't want to be there for me either.

On Monday morning, we had a school assembly in our newly renovated lunchroom. Exactly three weeks from the date of the shooting, the school awarded medals of honor to Luke and Faigyn. Foster's sister was so emotional she couldn't even accept her award. Before the principal could hand it to her, she ran off the stage in tears.

"Gosh, I need a break from all this," I mumbled.

I was sitting between Brittany and Meagan. They knew I had tried to avoid thinking about the whole thing, and I'd been successful in doing so, except when I saw or talked to Faigyn.

Several kids came up to the mike and talked about their fears. I wanted to get away and not have to deal with the troubles of it all. Talking about the issue was still tough for me.

"You know, next week is spring break," Brittany said, trying to cheer me up without getting us all in trouble for talking during assembly.

"Yeah," Meagan said quietly but eagerly. "We've reserved a hotel room in Panama City for four nights. It's right on the beach, and it's got two double beds. If you go with us, it would reduce the price for all of us."

It sounded great. But a trip with my friends over the school vacation was out of the question.

"What's with the long face?" Brittany asked. "What else were you gonna do over spring break?"

"I've got practice," I moaned. "Regionals and nationals

are coming up soon and I've got to be ready." My friends looked at each other and shook their heads.

"Hey," Brittany suggested, "I'm sure there must be a gym around there where you could practice. And if you go with us, we could take one day off the trip so you can get back early. Right, Meagan?"

"You bet," she agreed.

"Just think about it, OK?" Brittany begged.

As another speaker approached the podium and started talking about school violence, I could clearly see in my mind the blue waters of the Panama City Beach. The thought of going was pretty appealing.

The principal called Foster onto the stage. He used the opportunity to talk about how that gunman could have taken his life in an instant, but that was OK because he believed in a higher power. Foster encouraged everyone to get to know Christ for themselves.

"It's great being a ballplayer, it's great getting all As, and it's great having a boyfriend or girlfriend who can make you feel really special," he said. "But above and beyond all that, I know Someone who can make me feel better than hitting a grand slam ever could. That Someone can make you happier than seeing your name on the dean's list. He can fill you up and make you feel more special than any earthly relationship ever could."

He paused, and the room was still. No one moved or said a word. Even I was captivated by his moving testimony.

Foster continued. "The one I'm talking about is Jesus Christ. He is consistent. He's the same yesterday as He is today. If you don't know Him, I am pleading with you now to get to know who He is. He is right there at the door of your heart, knocking. I'm sure not advocating students shooting at other students. I hope I live long enough to see my great grandchildren. I know you all do too. But if tomorrow never comes, like it almost did for me three weeks ago today, then where is your hope?"

When Foster left the stage, he was given a standing ovation. My heart was beating fast because I was so proud of him. He was right. God doesn't ever let you down. It was evident in Foster's testimony that he had grown closer to Him since the shooting.

As the assembly ended, Meagan nudged me. "Well?" she said. "Aren't you gonna go congratulate him?"

I looked toward the front of the auditorium. Foster stood just below the stage, crowded by people. "I guess not," I said. "I'll talk to him later."

Throughout the rest of the day, as I thought more about those beaches in Panama City, I realized that I really did need a vacation. And maybe Foster and I didn't need to rush to be together again. It could be I'd be better off without any boyfriend for a while. And part of me knew Foster would be better off without a girlfriend.

The first meet without Coach Milligent was a success. All the girls, including myself, did well. I really missed his tough coaching, but Coach Weslyn's encouraging style proved to be effective.

Kirsten didn't perform with us. She had missed so many practices, the coaches thought it best that she sit out. But she was still there to cheer us on.

"Laurel, you did so good," she said to me after my beam routine, giving me a great big hug and an even bigger smile.

"Thanks," I said. She seemed overly friendly, and I didn't know what to make of it.

I spotted Coach Milligent from the corner of my eye. I really wanted to talk to him. I needed his brutally honest opinion of how I did. My goal wasn't just to be good. I wanted to be great!

"Thanks, Kirsten," I said, trying to get away.

"No, wait," she said, tugging on my arm. "What are you doing for spring break?"

"I don't know," I said. "Why?"

"I just wanted to see if you'd like to hang out with me for a couple of days. I really want to participate in the last meets, and I need to practice. I was wondering if you'd like to join me."

"I might not be here," I said. "My friends and I are thinking about going to Panama City."

"Really?" she squealed. "My friends are going there too. They invited me to join them. They even found a gym there so I can practice." Her enthusiasm dropped a notch. "I'm not sure if I'll go, though. I'd need a spotter."

"Well, I'm not sure if I'm going," I said, not wanting to make any commitments to this girl.

"Well, call me if you do," she said. "Maybe we can meet up in Panama and practice together."

Curiosity overcame me. "Kirsten," I asked, "why are you acting this way toward me?"

"What way?" she asked, sounding totally clueless.

I wasn't about to play games with this girl. "Why are you treating me so nice? It's not like we're friends."

She looked me in the eye. "I admire you," she said. "You are so good, you'll probably make it to the U.S. team. I just figured that instead of being against you, I want to be a positive force in your life." She paused. "I guess I should start by asking you to forgive me. I really would like us to be friends."

"Wow," I said, completely blown away. "Thanks, Kirsten. I'll give you a call about the trip when I decide what I'm going to do."

"Great!" She disappeared as fast as she had appeared.

I turned to look for Coach Milligent, but he was gone. I checked all around the complex, but couldn't find him anywhere. I went out to the parking lot and found him getting into his car.

"Wait, Coach!" I called as I ran up to him.

He turned at the sound of my voice. "Laurel," he said, "good meet."

"Thanks. I missed you out there."

"Oh? From what I saw, you didn't need me at all."

My heart skipped a beat. "Really? Was I that good?"

"Oh, yeah. Wouldn't I tell you if you weren't?"

I chuckled. "You've got a point there."

He grabbed the door handle of his car. "Well, you'd better get changed so you won't miss the bus."

I put a hand on his arm. "Thanks for coming and supporting us today, Coach."

He smiled. "You're welcome. It kind of feels like I've been on vacation."

"Coach Weslyn is great, but I need you. She does a fine job and all, but it's nowhere near the same."

His smile turned sad. "You might want to talk to your folks about that. You know what some of the parents are saying about me."

"Yeah, well, my parents never felt that way. You've coached me for a lot of years, and look at where I am now."

"Thanks," he said softly.

"No problem." I grinned at him, then hurried off to change.

When the team got back to Rockdale County Gym, I saw the family van waiting for me in the parking lot. Without even looking at the driver's side, I hopped in the passenger door and said, "Hi, Mom."

"Last time I checked, I was Dad," said my father's voice.

"Dad!" I said, really excited to see him. He almost never came to pick me up from practices or meets since he was so busy getting his sermons prepared and ministering to everyone in the congregation. But I was especially glad he'd come this time. I really wanted to go to Panama City with my friends, and I knew I would have to do some major talking to be given permission to go.

As he drove me home, I explained all the details I knew about the trip to him. He listened carefully, then said, "You've been through a lot lately. I'm not overly happy about this trip, but you do deserve a break. I'll talk to your mom. I don't think it'll be a problem for you to go."

I hugged his neck so hard he almost swerved off the road. "Sorry, Dad," I said with a huge grin on my face.

"I hope you girls will be more responsible than that on your trip. You can't go hugging your friend that way while she's driving."

"Oh, Dad! You know we'll be responsible."

He laughed. "Just checking."

"I love you, Dad."

"Don't try to butter me up, Laurel," he said, shaking his head. "I'm already considering your trip."

"No, really," I assured him with a straight face. "I really do love you."

I could tell he was taking my words to heart. "I love you too," he said.

"Which way am I supposed to go, Laurel? I don't know how to get to this girl's house."

"Turn down the music, Brittany," I said. "I already told you to turn left."

"I don't know why we have to take another person," Brittany whined.

"This girl is coming along," Meagan reminded her, "so Laurel can have someone to practice her gymnastics with, so we won't have to cut a day off our trip."

Brittany sighed. "You're right. So who is this girl, anyway?"

"Just a girl I know from Rockdale County Gym," I explained.

"A guy I used to date lives in this neighborhood," she said. "His name's Chevy Danson. He lives right there." She pointed to the house next door to Kirsten's.

"Really?" I said. "Well, Kirsten's house is right there." I pointed too.

"Oh, no," Brittany cried, slowing down the car in front of her house. "Are you serious?"

"What's the matter, Brittany?" Meagan asked.

"When Chevy and I started hanging out last year, he broke up with the girl he'd been dating for a long time. It was his next-door neighbor! She was so devastated when he told her they were through that she slashed his tires. When she found out the address of the girl he was dumping her for, she came over and slashed one of my tires too. For all I know, that crazy girl might try to kill me."

"Oh, please, Brittany," I said. "Maybe if you knew your boundaries better, we wouldn't be in this situation."

She rolled her eyes. "Oh, just go get your little friend!"

I got out of the car and slammed the door. I walked up to Kirsten's house and rang the bell. I wasn't about to let a little disagreement with Brittany ruin my vacation.

Kirsten opened the door, said good-bye to her mom, and walked with me to the car. Brittany opened the trunk and said, "Hi, I'm Brittany Cox. You slashed my tire last year."

Kirsten dropped her bag. "Oh, my gosh! I'm so sorry. Wow, you really are pretty. That must be why Chevy kept thinking about you."

Brittany suddenly changed her demeanor. "Oh, that's so sweet. I'm sorry too. I knew Chase was in a relationship at the time, but I didn't realize how much you liked him. Well, at least not until the tire-slashing incident."

Brittany and Kirsten laughed as they stuffed her suitcase into the trunk. I shook my head.

Half the way to Panama they talked about Chevy. When Brittany stopped for gas, she asked me if I wanted to drive so she could sit in the back and talk to Kirsten. I was happy to oblige.

When we pulled up in front of the hotel, Brittany called out, "Wow! This place looks great! What are we gonna do first?"

"Let's find the gym," I suggested.

"Not now," Brittany complained. "Let's have some fun first."

"We could go to the beach," Meagan said.

It took us about an hour to get settled into our room, and then we were ready to have a blast. We spent all day just walking along the beach strip, having a great time. Brittany and Kirsten started talking to a few guys, and around sunset, they invited us to a party in their penthouse suite.

I totally didn't want to go, and I told my girlfriends that. But they really wanted to. So I figured that since it was in the same hotel, I could stay until I wanted to leave and then get out of there.

We went back to our rooms to change clothes, put on makeup, and fix our hair. Brittany and Kirsten were giggling the whole time.

When we arrived at the suite, the place was packed with teenagers. There were beer bottles everywhere. When a girl I'd never met asked me if I wanted some Ecstasy, I decided this party was over for me.

I went to find my girlfriends to tell them it was time to go. I finally found them in a dimly lit corner. Meagan was chugging down a wine cooler, and Brittany and Kirsten were letting some guy give them puffs on his marijuana cigarette!

I took a deep breath and prayed. *Lord, what am I supposed to do? I didn't sign up for smoking on vacation.*

enjoying
what comes

I decided to go to the bathroom to cool off before I said anything to my girlfriends about their actions at the party. When I opened the bathroom door, I found a girl on her knees. "Oh, I'm sorry," I said.

As I started to close the door, she looked up and said in a sweet tone, "Guess I should have locked the door."

"Were you praying?" I asked.

"Yeah," she said defensively. "So?"

"Hey, I think it's great."

She got up and smiled at me. "I'm Hannah. Some friends of mine dragged me to this wild party, and I'm ready to get out of here. But I figure my friends will probably tell me to go back to the room by myself. So I was just praying for guidance."

I couldn't believe what I was hearing. I was just praying myself, and God led me to a girl who was in the same situation I was. When I told Hannah that fact, she was blown away too.

"God is so good, isn't He? Just when you think you're alone, you ask Him for help and He solves the problem, just like that."

"I'm Laurel Shadrach," I said, "from Conyers, Georgia."

"I'm from Montgomery, Alabama." She shook my hand. "Is Conyers near Atlanta?"

"Yeah, it's considered part of the greater Atlanta area."

"Listen," she said, "I didn't want to leave earlier because I didn't want to be by myself. But we don't have to stay in this smoky room. If you want, maybe we could head outside for an hour. Maybe by then our friends will be ready to go."

"That sounds great." The only thing I knew about this girl was her name and where she was from and that she loved the Lord. It wasn't a lot, but it was enough for me to trust my instincts and go with her. After all, we both believed it was divine intervention that had brought us together.

We ended up going back to the beach. We took off our shoes and carried them, letting the waves ripple over our feet.

"So, how many of your friends are here?" Hannah asked.

"There are four of us who drove down here together. But a lot of other people from our school came down this week too."

"Well, there are a whole bunch of people here. Unless you know what hotel your classmates are staying at, don't expect to even see them on the street. My friends and I have been here a week already, and we haven't seen one person from Jeff Davis."

"Who?"

Hannah giggled. "Our school, Jefferson Davis High. What school do you go to?"

"Salem High."

"Hey," she said, "I heard there's supposed to be a Christian bonfire down the beach."

"You're kidding! Really?"

"Yeah," Hannah said. "Want to check it out?"

"Sure!"

An hour later, I was having one of the best times of my life. The bonfire was a little piece of heaven. I was singing Christian songs with a group of people I had never met. It was a wonderful blessing.

As Hannah and I walked back to the hotel, we prayed for the confusion to be over at the penthouse.

"What if it's not?" I asked. "What if things are actually worse? How am I going to get my three friends out?"

"I don't know," she said quietly. "I guess what I have learned this week is that I may be my sister's keeper, but I can't live her life for her. I love my friends, and I wish they had the joy that you and I have. But they are on a totally different level. I love getting high on the Word of God, and if my friends can't understand that, they'll just have to deal with the consequences of their actions. If they get a hangover, they get a hangover. If they end up in some stranger's bed, then that's on them."

For some reason, her words made me more intent on getting back to my friends. I started running to the hotel as fast as I could through the sand.

"Hey," Hanna called after me. "Where are you going?"

"I'll meet you up there," I yelled back to her.

"Wait! Don't run alone!" In a few moments, she had caught up to me. "Why are you going so fast?" she asked, panting to keep up.

I couldn't explain to her that I had to get to my friend who had HIV before she ended up in bed with some guy without protection. I had thought about it earlier and was confident Brittany would never cross such a line. Not sober, anyway. But if she wasn't in her right mind, who knew what she would do? I had to be her keeper. I had to keep her from trouble if I could.

Hannah's hope that the party had died down was far from true. The exact opposite had happened. There were more people packed into the room, the music was even louder, and there was so much smoke I couldn't see a thing. By some miracle, I finally found Meagan.

"Laurel," she cried, her eyes and voice telling me she was completely out of it. "Hey, girl," she said.

"Where's Britt?" I asked urgently.

"Huh?" Her eyes tried to focus on my face.

"Where's Brittany?" I said louder, pulling her up by the collar.

"Britt? She's over there. She . . . she . . . she's over there with Kir- . . . Kir- . . . your friend."

"Kirsten?"

"Yeah," Meagan said, as if she'd just discovered electricity.

"I'll be right back," I assured her. "It's time to go home."

"Home?" she complained. "I don't have a curfew! I'm pulling an all-nighter here."

Meagan wasn't with a guy, so I wasn't too worried about her. I needed to find Brittany. I could talk to Meagan about her drunkenness later.

I scurried around the room trying to find Brittany but couldn't locate her anywhere. About the time I was ready to give up, I ran into Kirsten. She was more smashed than Meagan.

"Where is Brittany?" I asked.

"In there." Her hand weaved in the air and finally stopped when it pointed at a closed door down the hall. "She's with Sam."

My heart started beating faster. I sure hoped "Sam" was short for Samantha.

When I entered the room, I found three couples there, lying on a big bed. I felt so disgusted I wanted to throw up. Brittany was lying on top of the covers wearing only her undergarments, and she was starting to get rid of those.

"Brittany," I yelled. "Come on!"

"You're not my mom," she whined without looking up at me.

"What are you doing here, Brittany?"

The guy nearest her smiled at me. "Oh, let your friend have a little fun," he said. "She's a big girl." He leered at Brittany's chest.

"I'm not talking to you," I said forcefully. "Brittany, you can't do this. Let's go."

The guy talked to me again without taking his eyes off Brittany's nearly naked body. "If you're worried about protection, Little Mama, there's no need. I know how to make sure no babies come out, and nobody here has any diseases."

His comment made Brittany shoot right off the bed. She gathered her clothes, grabbed my arm, and dashed to the bathroom with me, where she immediately started crying. "Oh, my gosh," she cried. "What was I about to do? Laurel, thank you. Thank you!"

After I got her to drink some water and put her clothes on, I helped her down to our hotel room. Then I went back to get Kirsten and Meagan. Though it was hard being the responsible one, I was able to get all of my friends to safety. It was a good thing, too, because just as I was shutting our door, I saw flashing lights outside the window. I looked out and saw the Panama City Police racing into the hotel. With all the drugs and underage drinking, I knew everyone in that penthouse was going to get busted. I was glad Meagan, Brittany, Kirsten, and I were all safe inside our hotel room. I thanked God for being good to His children, even when they don't deserve it.

My friends and I spent the rest of our trip shopping and strolling the beach. Meagan and Brittany even went with Kirsten and me to the gym every day. We had a great time.

I arrived back home in the middle of the afternoon on Thursday. After I got most of my stuff unpacked, I decided to freshen up a little. Then my mom tapped on my bedroom door. "Feel like talking?"

"Sure," I said. "Come on in."

She took the white cotton ball I had in my hand and started removing my lavender nail polish for me.

"Mom, you don't have to do that."

"But I want to," she said. "Next year you won't be here for me to have the choice." I had to smile. "So," she asked, looking like she was about to burst, "did you enjoy your trip?"

"Oh yeah!" I said suddenly. "I got you something." I pulled my half-polished fingers out of Mom's hand and went over to my suitcase. I pulled out a set of crystal salt-and-pepper shakers filled with colorful sand that I'd kept wrapped up in a pair of clean socks. "This is so you can remember the first time you let me venture out on my own," I said, handing them to her.

My mother smiled at me and carefully set the shakers on my bed table. "Well, I'm glad you behaved responsibly. You came back in one piece and even got a tan." She started on my nails again. "Anything special about the trip you want to share with me?"

She was acting like one of my girlfriends, and I found it sorta strange and funny and endearing all at the same time. As she finished stripping the polish off my last fingernail, I asked, "Do you honestly think you can handle it?"

"Yes," she said, "I do." She grabbed a bottle of peach nail polish and wiggled it in front of me. I nodded my approval.

I thought about it for a minute, then decided to take the plunge. As she started to brush peach polish onto my fingernails, I said, "Well, at first I thought the trip would be horrible. When we got to Kirsten's house, I found out that Brittany used to date one of Kirsten's boyfriends."

"Really?" Mom said, her eyes bright. She was sure enjoying this girl talk.

"Yeah, but they got along right away."

"Then what happened?" she asked eagerly.

I hesitated. "Well, the first night was not one I am proud of."

"Why not?" She looked concerned, but not like she was going to jump all over my case, so I continued.

"Some guys invited us to a party, and some bad stuff happened there. But then some good stuff happened too." I told my mom about Hannah and the great time we had on the beach. "After that first night, we had prayer together every morning. It was really special."

"Did you get her number or address?" Mom asked, obviously thrilled that I had made a new Christian friend.

"Yeah," I said, "I did."

"What are you two ladies talking about in here?" my dad said as he came into the room.

"Dad!"

Careful not to ruin the wet polish on my nails, I wrapped my arms around his neck.

"So, tell me what you learned on vacation," he said.

I smiled. "I learned that I'm not just a follower, but a great leader."

His eyebrows raised. "You didn't know that already? Look at the way you lead in gymnastics."

I shrugged one shoulder. "That's different. I learned that a good leader can stay strong under pressure. It's not easy getting your friends to follow you."

He tilted his head. "So you kept your friends out of trouble, huh?"

I laughed. "I also learned that God shows up wherever you are. He's always there, just a prayer away. It was my first time away from home, and it was good to know I wasn't alone."

"We missed you so much," my mom said, wiping the corner of her eye.

"I missed you guys too," I said as I hugged them both.

The next day, Friday, was the last full day of vacation. I had gymnastics practice at Rockdale on Saturday and church

Sunday, then it was back to school on Monday. Brittany and Meagan took me mall-hopping all over Atlanta, trying to maximize our last free day. I didn't even know what we were shopping for.

"Cute outfits," Brittany explained. "All the spring stuff is on sale to make room for the summer stuff."

All I could think about was Foster. I desperately wanted to be with him. After our eighth mall, I just wanted to go home. Unfortunately, my friends didn't seem to want to respect my wishes.

"Come on, guys," I begged. "This is my last day off from everything, and you've got me running all over everywhere."

"Hold on a second," Meagan said suddenly. "I've got to check my messages." About three minutes later, she said, "Come on, let's go home."

"Oh, right," I complained. "Now that *you're* ready to go, we can, but when I was ready, we had to stay."

"Calm down," Meagan said. "Let's just go."

"Yeah," Brittany said, her arms loaded with shopping bags. "But let's all put on one of our new outfits first."

"What?" I complained. "I haven't even taken a bath."

"So what?" Meagan said.

"The longer it takes you to get ready, the longer it'll take to get home," Brittany teased.

We took our things into a public restroom and put on our new clothes. When Brittany finished dressing, she started styling my hair.

"Somebody tell me why I'm getting all dolled up," I said, feeling completely exhausted.

"To go home and crash," Meagan said. "Here, use my lipstick."

When we finally pulled into my driveway, not a single light was on inside the house. I breathed a sigh of relief. If no one was home, that meant I could enjoy a nice, relaxing evening of peace and quiet.

"I really have to use the bathroom," Meagan said, squirming. "Let me have the key while you guys get the rest of your bags out of the trunk."

"I only have one other bag," I said. But Meagan looked desperate, so I handed her the house key.

Brittany stood behind her closed trunk and looked at me. "You are a great friend," she said. "I almost did something really crazy this week and you stopped me. That guy had no idea he was lying down with someone who could kill him."

"Don't say that, Brittany."

"I'm just telling the truth, Laurel. Thank you. You're a true friend."

My heart broke for her. "You've got to quit thinking you're gonna die. People live with HIV all the time."

"I know," she said. "But thanks anyway." She opened the trunk. "Let me help you take this in."

"It's only one bag," I said. "I think I can handle it."

"I'm not going anywhere till Meagan finishes using your bathroom anyway," Brittany said, walking with me to the front door.

When I went inside and flipped on the lights, people suddenly jumped out from everywhere yelling, "Surprise!"

There were about sixty kids in my house, plus my parents. They took me downstairs where I found the entire area decorated with balloons and streamers, and there was lots of pizza and soft drinks. Luke played DJ, and he had some really cool Christian dance music going. No heavy metal or anything, which I knew my dad didn't like. The atmosphere was the exact opposite of the party at the penthouse. This one was under control.

The only problem was, I had no idea why everyone was having a surprise party for me. My birthday was more than two months away!

When everyone had settled into the party, I cornered my mom and dad. "What's this all about?" I questioned.

"Ask Brittany, Meagan, and Kirsten," Mom said with a smile. "They threw all this together."

My girlfriends walked up to me, each holding a glass of punch. Brittany hollered to get everyone's attention, then said, "Raise your cups to Laurel Shadrach. She is one girl who cares as much about her friends as she does about herself."

In unison the crowd cried out, "To Laurel!" They all took big gulps of soda and then returned to their conversations.

Just about everyone I knew was there, and even a lot of kids I didn't know. But when I looked around, I didn't see Foster. My heart sank. I was grateful to my girlfriends for putting all this together, and I was thrilled with how many people had come to my party. But the one person who was missing caused a deep void.

I sat on the carpeted steps and watched everyone having a good time. After a couple of minutes, Branson came up and sat next to me. "Hey, why the sad face? This is supposed to be a party for you."

I shrugged, not really knowing what to say to him.

"I heard you and your boyfriend broke up," he said with a sassy nod. "You need a guy like me."

I rolled my eyes.

"So what about prom?"

I had totally forgotten about prom, which was only a week away. The last time I'd spoken to Foster was our argument on the porch when Branson brought me home from the movies. Foster still hadn't returned my calls, so I didn't figure there was much chance he was going to ask me to prom. I hadn't even thought about a dress or shoes or anything. I'd been out shopping with my friends all day, and I hadn't even looked at prom dresses.

Thinking about shopping with my friends reminded me of why they had spent the entire day taking me around every mall in town. "Branson, I hate to cut you off," I said as I got up, "but I need to thank my friends for all this."

"Wait," he said, standing up behind me. "What about prom?"

I stopped and turned back to him. "What about it? Branson, we're not boyfriend and girlfriend anymore, even if Foster and I aren't together anymore either."

He touched my arm gently. "I may go alone. It would be nice if I could see you there."

"Sounds good to me," I said, then took off to find Brittany, Meagan, and Kirsten. They were standing at the buffet table refilling their plates with pizza. "Hey, you guys," I said. "Thanks for all of this."

Brittany gave me one of her big, toothy smiles. "It wasn't easy, was it Meagan?"

"No," Meagan said. "You're a hard person to surprise."

"Well, I really appreciate everything you did for me."

"It was our pleasure," Kirsten assured me.

"Mine especially," Meagan giggled.

"What do you mean?" I asked, knowing she was about to bust from some special secret.

"Well," she said, "Liam still hasn't asked me to prom, and it's coming up so soon, I finally asked him."

"You didn't!" I couldn't believe my shy friend had been so forward. "What did he say?"

"He said yes," she squealed with joy. I gave her a great big hug, and we bounced up and down together.

I looked around at my party and realized how blessed I was. This was going to be a great evening, with or without Foster.

"Hey," Kirsten said, "when are you going to open your presents?"

"Presents?" I said. "What are you talking about?"

My three friends turned me around and pointed to a long table in the corner. Sitting on top of a white linen tablecloth were stacks of brightly wrapped boxes covered with ribbons and bows. "You guys shouldn't have bought me presents," I said, although they could tell I wasn't really complaining. They followed me to the gift table. Everyone gathered around, and I started unwrapping presents and thanking all my guests. I got everything from Christian books and music to gag gifts, and I loved it all. Even more, I loved my friends who thought so much of me.

Now, this is a real party, I thought.

When I thought I had opened all my presents, a voice from behind me said, "You forgot one." It was a voice I'd longed to hear. Foster had come after all. I gave him a big kiss on the cheek and embraced him with a tight hug.

"Aren't you going to open his gift?" Brittany asked, pointing at a tiny silver box Foster held in his hands. When I opened it, I saw a pair of ruby earrings that matched the ring he'd given me on Valentine's Day.

Everyone cheered, then went back to mingling.

"Can we go somewhere and talk?" Foster whispered in my ear. We wandered off to a quiet corner.

"I missed you," I said before he could speak.

"Thanks for giving me some time," he said, holding my hand.

"It wasn't easy."

"I needed to think about why I acted so strangely when I saw you with Branson." He played with the ruby ring on my finger. "I know now it was pure jealousy and insecurity."

His tortured face broke my heart. "I'm so sorry. I don't know what it is with Branson, but the feelings I have for him are nothing close to the way you make me feel. I shouldn't have snuck around with him. You have nothing to be jealous about. I'm truly and completely yours." He gave me a warm hug. Still unsure of whether or not we were still boyfriend and girlfriend, I asked, "So, where does that leave us?"

He hesitated, as if he was giving my question serious thought. "Well," he finally said, "I really need a date for prom."

I jumped up and hugged him. Then we stared at each other for a long time without saying a word.

When my guests started to leave, Foster stood with me at the doorway while I said good-bye and thank you to everyone.

It had definitely been a day to remember.

Knowing that I was going to be away from Rockdale County Gym during spring break, I had asked Coach Milligent if he would give me some private coaching the week after I came back. Unfortunately, I hadn't taken prom into account when I made my request. He had agreed to work with me every night that week, but now I had another priority. I needed to find a prom dress!

I canceled our Monday practice, hoping I could find the perfect dress right away. But that didn't happen. I ended up canceling Tuesday, Wednesday, Thursday, and Friday as well. He got pretty upset with me, but I wanted to be beautiful for my special night with Foster. "I'll just work overtime the week after prom," I promised my coach.

My mom had offered to take me dress shopping, but I wanted to go with my friends. After five days of searching with Brittany and Meagan, Mom agreed to take me shopping on Saturday, the morning of the prom. To my amazement, I found five dresses that were beautiful and fit me perfectly. I ended up picking out a gorgeous fuchsia gown that complemented the ruby ring and earrings wonderfully. The combination made me look like a princess.

That evening, when I went to the bathroom to do some final primping, I found it occupied by a guy in a tuxedo. "Hurry up, Liam," I begged him. "Foster will be here any minute." When he turned around, I was shocked to see that the dressed-up guy was Lance. "Where are you going?" I questioned.

"Where are you going?" he asked back.

"To the junior-senior prom," I said in a snooty voice. "And you, my friend, are only a sophomore."

He shrugged. "When Branson found out you were going to the prom with Foster, he asked some junior girl, and her friend needed a date, so Branson asked me to come along." He smiled. "I didn't want to go, but duty calls."

"Do Mom and Dad know about this?"

"Hey, I don't need their permission to go out."

I rested one hand on my waist. "And where did you get the money for that tux? Are you gambling again?"

"I don't have to answer that," he said, giving me a rude look. Before I could say anything more, the doorbell rang. "Now, do whatever you have to do quick and get out of here," Lance grumbled. "I need to finish getting ready." He stormed out of the room.

I brushed my teeth, sprayed on a little perfume, and headed downstairs, where Foster and my parents were waiting.

"You look more beautiful than a sunset," Foster said as he pinned on my corsage. Mom took our pictures. Foster grabbed my hand and squeezed it. "I've got some surprises in store for you," he whispered as we walked out the front door.

"Bring it on," I teased. "I'm ready to start enjoying what comes."

having
an accident

Watch it, you jerk!" I yelled at Bo when he spilled punch all over my prom dress. Bo was Branson's best friend and we had never gotten along. He always resented the time I spent with Branson when we were dating.

"It's no big deal, Little Miss Perfect," Bo snarled at me. "The punch blends right in." His eyes were bloodshot and his breath reeked of alcohol.

I thought about picking Bo up and throwing him to the other side of the room. But I restrained myself. Foster had gone to the rest room, but I knew he'd be back any minute.

The prom was held at the Evergreen Resort Ballroom at Stone Mountain, and it couldn't have been more beautiful. Until Bo spilled punch all over my gown.

"This dress is fuchsia," I retorted, "not red. The punch does not blend in."

"Really?" Bo touched my dress with his punch-soaked hand to get a closer look. I pushed him back. His friends laughed, and I noticed Lance and Branson in the group. Being embarrassed fueled his temper. "Watch it, Laurel," he threatened under his breath. "I have no reason to be nice to you anymore."

"You were never nice to me."

He lowered his voice even more. "The way I treated you back then was a whole lot nicer than what's coming. So you'd better take heed."

"Ooh, threats," I said sarcastically. "I'm so scared."

He got up into my face, but my brother Lance came to my defense. "Hey, Bo," he said, "why don't you back off?"

Bo turned to Lance. "I like you," he said, "but your sister is out of control." Then he went back to join the group.

"I'll see you guys in a sec," Lance said to his friends as he walked me in the opposite direction.

"Why are you hanging out with those losers, Lance?" I asked as we neared a quiet corner.

"I don't need a lecture, Laurel."

"That guy is drunk. He's a bad influence."

"Well, if you know he's been drinking, then why are you pushing his buttons? Go enjoy Foster and leave us alone. We've got some big action planned tonight."

I peered at him with sisterly concern. "What big action?"

"Oh, you'll see." He grinned. "Salem High has a lot of excitement coming this evening."

Before I could say anything more, he strolled back to his group of guys. As I watched him, Foster came up behind me. "Hey, I've been looking for you. You weren't where I left you."

"I need to go to the restroom," I said. "Look at my dress." When I glanced down I almost started crying.

"How did you do that?"

"I didn't! Some jerk bumped into me."

"It doesn't look that bad," he said. "Hardly noticeable."

I smiled at my sweet, understanding boyfriend. "I still want to see if I can rinse it out," I said. He nodded. "Hey," I said, looking at the two glasses of punch in his hand, "there was something more than punch in that guy's cup. I could smell it."

He looked confused. "I took a sip of my drink and it tasted fine."

"I think they brought their own stash," I said.

He shook his head. "Go take care of your dress. I'll wait here for you."

"OK," I said. "I'll be right back."

I used soap, water, and paper towels to blot the punch stain, but it could still be clearly seen. When I heard the bathroom door open, I turned the opposite way so whoever was coming in wouldn't see me fixing my dress and crying. But when I looked up, I saw Robyn in the mirror. I turned around and tried to hug her, but the response I got was one of complete disgust.

"Robyn, what's wrong?" I asked.

"Don't even go there with me, girl," she said in a major huff.

I couldn't believe she was talking to me that way. "What did I do?"

"Talk to this," she said, shoving her hand into my face.

"Robyn, what's going on? I thought we were friends. You're acting like we're enemies."

"I don't know if we're enemies," she said, "but we're definitely not friends. I heard about the big party you had a week ago. You didn't even think to invite me, did you? Wouldn't want a black girl at your silly white party, huh? So don't go trying to be my friend here at school when I'm not a good enough friend for you to invite to your house for a party. I don't have time for that. Excuse me." She pushed me away and headed into the nearest stall.

I thought back to my party and realized Robyn was right. There wasn't a single black face at my house that night. I hadn't thought about it at the time, but Robyn should have been at my party. She was one of my really good friends. Why hadn't I missed her? Why didn't I wonder where she was?

When Robyn came out and went to the sink to wash her hands, I started fixing my dress again, as a diversion to calm my nerves. "I want to apologize," I said softly, too embarrassed to look her in the eyes. "I didn't notice you at my party. But that doesn't mean you're not my friend."

"You didn't invite me."

Her sad voice made me look up. "It wasn't my call. It was a surprise party. Believe me, Robyn, if I'd had anything to do with it, you would have been invited."

Her lips formed a smirk. "When you found out about the party, you could have called me. But you didn't. I bet you didn't even ask your friends why they didn't invite me."

"No, I didn't," I admitted, "and I really am sorry." We looked at each other for a long moment. Then Robyn took the paper towel from my hand and started working on the stain on my dress.

"I'm glad you wanted to be at my party," I said.

"I'm glad to hear you didn't plan the party." She scrubbed my dress for a while in silence.

"So, are you here with Jackson?"

"Yeah," she said. "We're doing great. We had a talk. I'll have to tell you about it. Who are you here with?"

"Foster," I said proudly.

"There," she said, tossing the paper towels into the wastebasket. "You're all fixed up."

I looked down and saw that the stain was completely gone. "Thanks," I said warmly.

Robyn moved me to the hand dryer and punched it on. She held the fabric under the hot air, and before I knew it, I couldn't even tell there'd been a stain there.

I hugged Robyn. "I do care about you. We'll have to hang out soon."

"You bet," she said with a smile.

I immediately went over to Foster and pulled him to the

dance floor. A slow song was playing, and I didn't want to miss it. I slipped into his arms, closed my eyes, and started swaying to the music. But after a few seconds, I felt Foster's body tense up.

I opened my eyes and saw Branson standing beside us. "Whoa, partner," he said, "you shouldn't let your girl get that far away from you." He slid between us and asked, "You don't mind, do you?"

Foster pulled away, nodded, and extended his hand. "Go ahead."

Branson took me in his arms, and Foster faded into the crowd. "Why did you do that?" I said, struggling to get out of his tight embrace.

He pulled me closer. "Because I wanted to dance with the most beautiful girl in the room." He closed his eyes. "Mmm, you feel great."

"Branson—"

"Laurel, you being with Foster is a joke. He doesn't even know how to make you feel good."

"You're drunk," I said.

"No, I'm not," he responded, looking me in the eye. "I've had a few drinks, but I know what I'm saying."

I sighed. "Branson, why do you have to drink all the time?"

"Why do you have to get on my case all the time?" he said, an edge of anger creeping into his voice. "Let's just enjoy this song." He pulled me close again and started rubbing my back.

"Stop it," I said. I looked around and found Foster. "My boyfriend is watching."

"Then I might as well show him how it's done," he said. "I've seen you trying to teach him."

"What are you talking about?"

"Every time you walk up to the guy he walks in the opposite direction. What's with that, Laurel? You can't be happy in that kind of relationship."

The slow song ended, but a faster one started right away, and Branson continued to dance with me. He definitely had rhythm, and dancing with him made me feel light and graceful. And sexy. Though I hated to admit it, there was still a passion between us.

I melted into the music and the excitement of dancing in Branson's arms. As we floated across the dance floor, my mind went into a kind of trance. When the song ended, he moved in to kiss me. I started to give in to it, but was pulled out of my trance when Foster said, "What are you doing, Branson?" I blinked at him, trying to clear my mind. "That's enough dancing. Come on, Laurel."

Foster led me to the other side of the room. I couldn't breathe. Branson had really got me going.

"That guy sure knows how to push my buttons," Foster grumbled. Then he held me close and kissed me on the cheek. "I guess it's understandable. Who would want to lose you?" Foster glared at Branson, who was watching us.

Foster started kissing my lips. Branson stormed over to Bo. His little group left the ballroom, and as soon as they did, Foster took his hands from around me. "Do you want to sit?" he asked.

I nodded. For the next thirty minutes we just sat at the table and watched other people dance. "We should get our picture taken," I said.

"Yeah, let's do that."

After we finished posing for the camera, the principal announced that it was time to name the prom king and queen. Meagan and Liam found their way to us, and she whispered in my ear, "You know you're going to get it."

"I don't think so," I said, shaking my head. "I was already Homecoming Queen."

"That's why you'll win. For the last five years the prom queen has always been the homecoming queen."

"This year's king is," our principal announced, "Branson Price. Branson, come on up!"

The crowd screamed. I wanted to be up there so badly. But when the principal pronounced Brittany Cox as the queen, I couldn't have been happier for my friend.

"That's OK," Meagan said. "You didn't want it anyway. Yea, Brittany!"

When Branson and Brittany reached the platform, the principal asked, "Do you guys have anything you want to say?"

"I just have one thing," Branson said as he took the mike. "Doesn't our prom queen look beautiful?" He dipped her and kissed her with what looked like serious desire. For some weird reason, I felt extremely jealous.

The principal broke up the little display on the stage and insisted that we all go back to dancing. I looked at Foster with tears in my eyes and realized there was something seriously wrong between us.

"You like that guy, don't you?" Foster said, his voice sad and quiet.

"No," I protested. "Why would I like him?"

"I don't know why, Laurel. But when your eyes water just because you can't be up there with that jerk, I realize that being in a relationship with you is clearly a waste of my time."

"I don't like him!"

"Who are you trying to convince?" he asked. "Me or you?" Foster started to turn away from me.

"Wait," I said, grabbing his arm. "You've got to understand. I want to be with you."

"That's not my problem," he said as he jerked away and stormed off.

I turned around and found Meagan nearby. I rushed to her, put my head on her shoulder, and started crying. "How did things get so messed up?" I whimpered.

"It's OK, Laurel," she said, rubbing my back.

I let her words and her hug of friendship calm my sobbing. In my heart I knew Meagan was right. It was going to be OK. I didn't know how, but I knew God would cause everything to turn out all right.

"C'mon, you guys," Brittany said as she grabbed my hand and Meagan's.

"Where's everybody going?" Meagan asked.

When I looked up from Meagan's shoulder, I saw people running out of the building in a frenzy of excitement.

"There's going to be a car race outside," Brittany answered, bouncing with anticipation.

"So what?" I said. "Car races are stupid. Why would I want to see this one?"

Brittany tilted her head, raised a brow, and placed a hand on her hip. "Maybe because your brother is going to be in it."

I ran outside. When I reached the side of the road, completely out of breath, I looked around frantically but couldn't find Lance anywhere. Then I saw Bo's white Chevy Blazer with four guys packed inside. Branson sat in the front passenger seat, and Lance was in the back. Alongside the Blazer was a black Chevy El Camino with a bunch of kids I recognized from our main sports rival, Rockdale High.

I looked down the road in the direction the cars were facing. A short distance away, the pavement curved along the side of a mountain slope. I couldn't see any farther, but someone behind me said there was a white finish line on the far side of the curve.

Someone in the crowd shouted, "Go!" Immediately, the two cars sped off, leaving a cloud of smoke from the tires and the pungent odor of burnt rubber.

"No!" I screamed.

"Laurel, it's OK," Brittany said, shaking her head. "They'll be fine."

"No, it's not OK," I retorted. "They've been drinking!"

Brittany and Meagan ignored me and followed the crowd down the street to watch the racing cars. I spotted Liam and grabbed his arm. "Liam, they've been drinking," I panted.

"I know," he said, his eyes wide. "I tried to stop Lance."

"I've got a really bad feeling about this."

"Me too." Liam put his arms around me and held me close. It was the first time the two of us had been on the same wavelength in a long time. I hated the fact that worrying about Lance's safety was what brought us together.

Before I could even begin to pray, I heard a horrific crashing sound. It frightened me even more than the gunshots I'd heard in the hallway at school.

The crowd started running in the direction of the crash. When I rounded the curve, I saw one of the cars smashed into the side of the mountain. It was the black El Camino.

"Help!" someone behind me screamed.

I turned around and saw a crowd gathered at the edge of the cliff. I cut through the tight knot of people and looked over the mangled side rail. Bo's Blazer was perched precariously a few feet down the mountainside. I couldn't see any movement from inside the vehicle.

We all stared for what seemed like an eternity, but was really only a few minutes before an ambulance arrived. I heard people behind me saying that the four guys in the car that had hit the mountainside were fine. I watched hysterically as rescue workers tried to figure out how to get to the Blazer that had gone over the cliff.

Foster approached from behind me and wrapped his arms around me. "Everything's going to be all right," his calm voice assured me. "I'm sure it's not as bad as it looks." He held me closer and whispered, "They'll survive having an accident."

f o u r t e e n

coping
with reality

"Stand back, kids! We've got to clear this area," a police-man ordered in a harsh voice.

None of us abided by his wishes right away. We all wanted to see what was going on. But we moved aside for the paramedics. If there was any chance of survival for any-one in the car, we knew the passengers would need to be tended to immediately.

Rescue workers from two fire trucks, three ambulances, and six police cars stood at the edge of the cliff discussing the best way to get those guys out of the car. As four gur-neys were carefully taken down the hillside, my parents ar-rived. My father's arms replaced Foster's around me.

"What's going on?" he asked, his voice shaking.

"I don't know, Dad! I don't know anything."

"It's going to be OK, Laurel," Mom said, but she didn't sound completely convinced.

I held my breath as the first gurney was pulled up the

cliff and taken to a waiting ambulance. My mother took over holding me while Dad and Liam approached the rescue workers to get more information.

"He's not conscious," I heard one of the paramedics say. I edged my way through the people gathered around the ambulance and saw the face of the person on the gurney. My heart skipped two beats. It was Branson.

"He's dead," I yelled hysterically. Every part of my body seemed to stop working. I was unable to breathe, my heart was pounding like mad, and I felt a massive headache coming on. This couldn't be happening.

I shoved people out of my way and pushed through the crowd. "He can't be dead," I cried, tears streaming down my face. "I love him!"

As the paramedics loaded the gurney into the ambulance, Branson's mom reached out to me. We leaned into each other, then collapsed onto the pavement together, neither of us strong enough to hold up the other.

The feeling of devastation that filled my soul made me realize how much I cared for this man and how much I wanted him in my life.

"We've got a pulse!" a paramedic yelled from inside the ambulance.

Mrs. Price cried harder. Inwardly, I thanked the Lord.

"We've got to get him to the hospital," the paramedic yelled. As a second rescue worker started to close the doors, he asked Branson's mother if she wanted to ride with him.

"Yes, please," she said. Then she turned to me. "Thank you, Laurel. I'll tell Branson you were here. I hope your brother is OK." The rescue worker helped her into the back of the ambulance and it drove off, lights blazing and siren blaring.

I looked back at the cliff and saw a guy I didn't recognize being helped over the edge by a rescue worker. He was gingerly holding his left arm with his right one, but other than that, he didn't seem hurt. When he reached safety, he started screaming, "He's hurt really bad! You've got to get to him!"

My hand flew to my mouth to stifle a scream. Mom crumpled to the ground, sobbing. My father clasped his hands together and looked up to the sky. Following Dad's lead, I prayed aloud, "Lord, please help my brother."

Seconds later, another gurney appeared over the edge of the cliff, and my brother was on it. His head was bleeding badly from a gash over his left eye, but he was conscious. A paramedic assured us that after a few stitches he would be as good as new. That meant the person who was hurt badly wasn't my brother. It had to be Bo.

Mom and both of my other brothers followed the ambulance to the hospital in the family van. Dad and I stayed around to see what had happened to Bo. As we waited, I realized that my prayer had really been selfish. Although Bo and I didn't get along, I didn't want him to die.

I looked around and noticed the crowd hadn't thinned out. No one could go home because everyone wanted to know how Bo was. I didn't see Foster in the crowd, so I decided to try to find him. "I'll be right back," I told my dad.

"I'd rather you stay beside me," he said. "I don't need to worry about you too."

"I'll be right back," I assured him. "I have to find Foster."

He nodded and I started to take off. But before I could get anywhere, Bo was brought up on a stretcher. The white sheet covering most of his body had turned almost completely red. Bo's arms and torso were shaking uncontrollably.

"He must be in shock," my dad commented.

Bo was immediately put into the last ambulance, and his parents got in too. Just before the doors closed, we all heard his mother scream, "No!"

The word lingered in the air as the ambulance sped off into the night.

A policeman started gathering the remaining spectators

around him. "This started out as a night you all wanted to remember," he said, "but it will go down as a night you will want to forget. Tragedy was here this evening. Eight young men were involved in a car accident, and four of them were badly hurt, all because of senseless drinking and driving. The night isn't over, but whatever plans you had, I suggest you cancel them. Go home. Spend time with your families. And pray for these young men. Especially the one who left last. He lost both of his legs, and he's fighting for his life."

We all stood there in a daze, sheer terror written on everyone's faces.

"We can't go back in time and change what occurred here tonight. But you can make sure this never happens again. Consider this your warning. I don't want any more incidents like this in Rockdale County. I would rather escort you to jail than to the morgue."

My dad approached the policeman and said a few words to him privately. Then the officer announced, "Rev. Shadrach is going to pray for everyone. His son was in the accident."

"I hope you all heard what the officer said," my dad began, "and I hope you heed his words." He looked around at the quiet group. "Let's pray." He closed his eyes. "Father, we thank You for Your grace. We ask that You be with these young people and get them home safely. Thank You for allowing eight young men to continue breathing. Please touch them with Your healing power. We particularly pray for Bo. I'm sure he has no idea yet that he will never be able to walk again. We ask You to give him the courage to know that even though his legs are gone, his life is not over. We love You and we praise You. In Jesus' name we pray. Amen."

As people started heading for their cars, Foster found me. I hugged him tightly and asked, "Where did you go?"

"I had to get away to think," he whispered. "And I wanted to give you some space." His voice broke. "I'm glad to see that your brother and the one who has your heart are both

OK." He released me and walked away. I wanted to go after him and tell him that my heart belonged to him. But for some reason, I couldn't do that. All I could think about was getting to the hospital.

———————————

All four of the boys involved in the accident were still at the hospital when Dad and I arrived in the Seville. Although it was late, visiting hours were open to family. But I didn't immediately head for Lance's room. Instead I hovered near Branson's room. I peeked through the open door and saw him resting in the bed. His mother was asleep in a chair next to him.

Something drew me to Branson's side. I grabbed his hand and stroked it as gently as I could. "I don't know what I would have done without you," I said.

His eyes fluttered. "Laurel," he whispered. "Where am I?" He tried to move, then cried out, "My head!" He tried to grab his temples but couldn't because his arms had tubes attached to them. Branson's mom woke up and looked at me, her eyes still dazed. I found the button to the nurses' station and pressed it. Within moments a woman in a white uniform rushed into the room.

"Who are you, Miss?" she asked as she examined Branson.

"This is my son's friend," Mrs. Price explained, rising from the chair.

As the nurse continued to check out Branson, Mr. Price came into the room. His clothes were rumpled, and his shirt was buttoned wrong.

"Where have you been?" Mrs. Price grumbled.

"I got here as fast as I could." When he drew closer, I smelled alcohol on Mr. Price's breath.

Mrs. Price stepped back a few feet. "I don't even want to know where you've been. Your son could have died while you were out doing God knows what!" She brushed past him and left the room.

"Honey, wait!" he called after her. I wanted to follow her, but I couldn't leave until I knew Branson was all right.

The nurse explained to Mr. Price that Branson had suffered a severe concussion and some internal bleeding, but everything was under control. The nurse continued talking softly, but that was enough information for me. I left to find Branson's mom.

I found her in the ladies' room, standing in front of the mirror crying. "He's going to be fine," I told her.

"I hate having to go through this all alone," she said, turning to me. "It's like I'm a single parent. Our marriage is in trouble, and I thought being apart would be the best thing, at least for a while. But it really hurts."

I stretched out my arms and gave her a warm embrace. Without even asking her if I could pray, I started talking to the Lord. "Father, we thank You for Your grace and mercy. Thank You for times of trouble because they make us realize that we need You to see us through. I pray for Mrs. Price. Show her that You are a miracle worker and that she can put her hope and trust in You. We love You, Lord. Amen."

Branson's mom sniffled and wiped her eyes with a tissue. "You should go check on your brother. I'll be fine. Give your family my love."

"Are you sure you'll be all right?" I asked.

She nodded. "You're a sweet person, Laurel. My son is just like his father. He doesn't know a good girl when he has one."

We left the bathroom and went in separate directions. As I walked toward my brother's room, I realized that instead of walking through a hospital, I could have been walking through a funeral home. I was grateful that God had saved my brother and his friends because they needed to get their lives together. If they had died that night, I had no idea where their souls would go.

As I opened the door to Lance's room, I saw stitches in my brother's head and tears in my parents' eyes.

"Where have you been?" my father asked as he stretched out his arms to me.

I walked into my dad's comforting embrace. "I was checking on Branson."

"How is he?"

"He's going to be OK, thank the Lord. How's Lance?"

"I feel terrible," Lance moaned from his bed. "I'm so sorry, Mom." Tears covered my brother's face. "You were right, Laurel," he said. "I've got a problem." He looked at Mom and Dad. "I think I'm an alcoholic. I told you guys I wouldn't touch the stuff anymore, but I did. I feel so ashamed."

"Well, Son," Dad said, "that's the first step to recovery. Admitting you have a problem. This accident was a wake-up call for all of you boys."

"How is everybody else?" Lance asked.

"They're still alive," my father confirmed. "But none of us ever knows when our last breath will be. So we all need to live each moment for the Lord. He can make a blessing even out of this situation, but you've got to trust Him to do it."

My dad was right. This tragedy had already brought us closer together as a family. It was turning out to be a true treasure from God.

The next morning, the sensation of someone stroking my hair woke me. I opened my eyes and saw my father's father standing over me.

"I'm sorry," Grandpa said, "I didn't mean to startle you."

"How did you get here?" I asked groggily.

"Your dad picked me up from the airport."

"What time is it?"

"Nine o'clock."

I started to sit up. "I've got to get ready for church."

"Your dad said you all had a pretty late night. He thought you might want to sleep in."

I sat up in my bed and hugged him.

"I'm glad to hear Lance is all right," he said. "But I've got to try to talk some sense into that boy. If he would have listened to me at Christmas, this all could have been avoided." He patted my knee. "Anyway, I made us some muffins and fresh-squeezed orange juice, so come on downstairs whenever you're ready. It's just the two of us this morning. Your dad's at the church, and the rest of the family is already at the hospital."

When I got down to the kitchen and started enjoying breakfast with my grandfather, I broached the subject that had been on my mind all night. "Grandpa, I think I have feelings for my ex-boyfriend."

"Is that the boy you went to the prom with last night?"

"No, that was my current boyfriend. But he understands."

His bushy white eyebrows rose. "He understands that you like another guy?"

"Yeah."

He shook his head, then asked, "Well, who is this other guy?"

"He was in the car with Lance," I said quietly. "His name is Branson."

"If he was intoxicated like the other boys in that accident, he doesn't sound like a very moral young man to me."

"Oh, that's not true," I said. "In many ways he's a lot like Lance. He understands the seriousness of his actions."

Grandfather took a bite of his muffin and thought for a moment. "Before you get into anything with this Branson fellow, you'd better be sure you like him for who he is and not who you hope he will turn out to be."

I knew my grandfather was right. I had to look deep within my heart and analyze my true feelings.

A glance at the clock told me I still had time to make it to church if I left right away. I'd miss the worship songs but could still get there in time for my dad's sermon. I couldn't remember a single Sunday when at least one of our family members wasn't in the congregation giving Dad some support. Not wanting this Sunday to be any different, I decided that going late was better than not going at all.

As I slipped into the back row, my father began his sermon. "All of my family members are at the hospital right now. As some of you may have heard, there was a terrible car accident last night at Salem High School's prom." I heard several people gasp. "I'm pleased to report that all of the young men involved in the accident are still alive, although some are in very serious condition and desperately need our prayers."

My dad paused to calm his emotions, which were very close to the surface. "The topic of my sermon today is 'Life: Only If You Know Him.'"

His sermon title seemed particularly appropriate for me. I was glad I had come. I knew God was going to use my daddy to heal my heart.

"Last night's accident was caused by substance abuse. When you love the Lord, you don't need that kind of high. You can get high on the love God gives. The only thing that matters is pleasing God. At the beginning of the year, both my son and my daughter were tempted with the same thing. My wife and I prayed for them. One of them grew stronger and conquered that area, and the other one is now ready to do the same. Folks, you don't need a fix or a bottle to make you happy. You need the everlasting joy that only God can give you."

As my dad continued to preach, I thought of all the times God had rescued me in my life. The Lord was everything to me, and knowing that calmed all my fears.

After the service I headed to the front of the sanctuary to tell my father how much his sermon had meant to me. But partway down the aisle, I saw something that made me stop. Foster McDowell was walking toward the church doors one aisle over. As much as I wanted to see my father right then, I knew my boyfriend and I needed to talk. I cut through an empty pew and caught up with him. "Hey, can we talk for a second?"

He didn't even look at me. "There's really not much to say."

"What does that mean?" I asked, grabbing his arm.

He led me to a quiet corner of the foyer. "Laurel, I care about you, and I want you to be happy. So I'm taking myself out of the equation. It's obvious you still care about Branson. I want to see what happens between you and him if I'm not involved."

I swallowed hard. "Does this mean we're breaking up?"

"Yeah," he said with a sad nod. "But don't worry. If we find our way back to each other, that's great. If not, then that's obviously for the best."

I blinked. "Are you sure you're OK with this?"

He shrugged, then his shoulders returned to their slouched position. "It's not easy dealing with the truth," he said, "but I'm sure I'll be fine. I'm just coping with reality."

f i f t e e n

getting
it finally

O h, I get it," I said after chasing Foster to keep him from leaving the church.

Foster crossed his arms over his chest. "You get what?"

"You think you're better than me," I said.

"What are you talking about?"

"You're willing to give up your happiness so I can be happy, right?"

He rolled his eyes. "Well, maybe if I had some bad boy in me, you'd be all into me the way you are with Branson."

"Foster," I said, "I really do care about you."

He looked deep into my eyes and spoke softly. "Laurel, you've made your choice. Now both of us just have to live with it." A tear trickled down his face.

"I care about you so much," I whispered, feeling tears coming to my own eyes.

"Just like you can't get Branson out of your head, I won't be able to get you out of mine. But we're on different tracks.

I want more from you than you're ready to give right now. You like both Branson and me, but if you have to make the choice—and you do—I end up the loser." He touched my arm. "I'm not angry with you, and I don't think I'm better than you. I'm just withdrawing from the competition. Let's just make a clean break, OK?"

I shook my head. "Foster, saying good-bye this way just doesn't seem right."

"I know," he said, "but what else can we do?" He hugged me and kissed me on the cheek. I couldn't watch him walk away. So I decided to be the one to leave first.

As I turned back toward the sanctuary doors, I prayed, *Lord, please be with this wonderful guy. Thanks for letting me know him.*

Was I making a mistake? I sure hoped not. I knew things between Foster and me would forever be different. It broke my heart, but Foster was right. It had to be done.

My father was still talking to parishioners in the front of the sanctuary. Before I could reach him, Brittany jumped into my pathway. Meagan stood right beside her.

"What are you guys doing here?" I asked.

"With everything that's been going on," Brittany said, "I thought I needed to come to church. I called Meagan, and she said I could tag along with her."

"That's great," I said, beaming with joy.

"So, what's going on with you and Foster?" Brittany asked. She looked like she couldn't wait to get in on some bit of juicy gossip.

"I don't really want to talk about it right now," I said. "I need to go see my father."

I tried to walk around them, but Brittany got back in front of me. "Laurel, I've been doing some soul searching lately, and I realize now that you still like Branson, and he still likes you. I don't know much about God, but I know He spoke to me this morning."

"He did?" I asked.

"Laurel, I think you should find your way back to Branson," she said with determination in her voice.

"Why would you say that?" I questioned.

"Because I care about you, my friend, and I want you to be happy. You and Branson are supposed to be together."

The three of us started hugging and crying. "God loves you, Brittany," I said.

"Yeah," she replied, beaming. "I know."

———————————

When I arrived at the hospital, I went straight to my brother's room. As I neared the open doorway, I heard Liam and Lance talking and bonding. I wanted to be part of that moment, but I knew Liam and Lance needed some time alone.

I walked down the hall to Branson's room. When I passed through the doorway, I saw him weeping. I fled to his side. "Branson, what's wrong?"

"Bo lost his legs," he said, his words broken by deep sobs. "He's never going to be able to walk again."

"I heard," I said quietly, taking his hand.

"I know you and Bo never got along, but he's my friend."

"Branson, I'm devastated about his loss too. But praise the Lord, he's still alive. I don't know what I would have done if you hadn't been all right." I leaned over his bed, and Branson wrapped his arms around me. He squeezed me tight for several minutes as tears slid down his face into the pillow. When he finally loosened his grip on me, I straightened, then put both of my hands around one of his.

Branson looked at me with a devastated expression. "Bo was accepted to go to Texas A&M University. He was going to play pro ball for them. And now that's never going to happen. He's in a coma right now, so he doesn't even know his future is over. I'd give up everything to give him back his legs. This is all my fault."

I'd never heard Branson talk like this. It was like he was

changing right before my eyes. I squeezed his hands. "You made a mistake, but it's done. You survived, and so did your friend. Bo doesn't have everything he used to have, but he's still valuable. You can't beat yourself up over something that's already done. If you both learn from this, that's the best thing that can happen."

He stared at the wall, deep in thought. Then he turned back to face me. "I have learned some things," he said. "I know now that life is about more than doing everything you want and doing it all your own way. There are rules for a reason."

Branson was right. He and Brittany were both learning the hard way that God gives us rules to protect us. When we go against those rules, sometimes the consequences are almost too much to bear.

"This has also taught me to live for the moment. Time is precious." He pulled me closer. "I've wanted to do this for a very long time." His lips touched mine gently, and only for a brief moment. Then he pulled away. "I've missed you. I don't know where things stand with you and Foster, but I want you back in my life. I want to be your boyfriend again. I want to grow and learn about the Lord you love. Please tell me you want that too."

His words soothed my soul. Branson had a desire to be right with God, and that was exciting to me. But I didn't want to give him an answer about what our future might hold until I saw that his decision was real, not just brought on by his recent traumas.

"I'll check on you every day while you're in here," I said gently. Then I kissed his forehead and left the room.

When I returned to Lance's room, I found him alone, dressed in his own clothes, sitting on the side of the bed.

"Are you ready to go home?" I asked.

"Yeah," he said with a big smile. "Mom and Liam are checking me out." He gave me a big hug. "Thank you, Laurel," he said. "I've given up drinking for good. I've also given up gambling. I want to follow God completely now. But I know I can't do it by myself. I'm going to need your help."

I hugged him back. "I'm so proud of you."

Mom and Liam came in, and Liam helped a nurse get Lance into a wheelchair. "Standard procedure," she explained when Lance complained that he could walk out of the hospital on his own.

As Liam pushed Lance's chair down the hall, Mom pulled me aside. "Laurel, your father and I are very proud of you. I know being a teenager is difficult. Even when you try to do the right thing, something always comes along to tempt you." She put her arm around my shoulder. "I don't want you to feel like you can't come to me when that sort of thing happens."

"Thanks, Mom," I said. Her words really made me feel good about myself.

"I love you, Laurel. You're very special to me."

There were many uncertainties still ahead for me, but I did know one thing: I wanted to follow God. I was going to live my life for Him. The Lord would supply all of my needs. I was glad God sent His only Son to die on the cross for me. There was no greater joy than for me to surrender my life back to Him. God was all I needed. I was truly thankful. I knew in my heart that I was getting it finally.